LETHAL FORCE

LETHAL FORCE

THE SILENCER SERIES BOOK 11

MIKE RYAN

Cover Design: The Cover Collection

Edited By: Graham Toseland

1

Recker left the office to go home, already knowing he was in for a rough night. Mia was taking another nurse's shift, on top of her own, so she was working a double, and wouldn't get done until around seven in the morning. Anytime Mia wasn't there at night, Recker seemed to have a tougher time of it. Not only did he have a harder time getting to sleep without her being next to him, it seemed his dreams were even worse when she wasn't there. Maybe it was just because she had a way of calming him down after he woke up from what seemed like a nightly occurrence and knowing she wouldn't be there this time was stroking his fears even worse than usual.

Recker's fears were rightly founded, as even though he put his head down on a pillow at eleven o'clock, he didn't drift off to sleep until about two. He tossed and turned, unable to turn his mind off from thinking horrible thoughts. And it was another rough one for him once his eyes closed for good. The nightmares started only a few minutes after falling asleep.

Recker walked into the cafeteria at the hospital, sitting at his usual table as he waited for Mia to come down from the pediatric wing. Almost immediately after sitting down, he saw her beautiful face walk in. Recker stood up and kissed his black-haired beauty once she got to the table.

"So, what's this about?" Mia asked. "What's the big emergency that couldn't wait until I got home?"

"I just had to call you and let you know."

"Know what?"

"I think I'm done with it all."

"You are?"

"Yeah," Recker said. "I'm just done. I'm tired. The constant danger, the injuries, the physical toll, the mental damage, I just can't do it anymore."

"Stop. Don't talk like that. You know you don't mean it. It's just the dreams that are doing it to you."

"No, I'm really serious. I'm not sure I wanna do this anymore."

"It's just the dreams playing tricks with your mind, Mike."

"This isn't a dream talking. It's how I really feel. I just wanna rest. For good."

"You can't rest. If you rest, you'll die. You need this to keep going."

"All I need is you," Recker said. "This is what you've always wanted, isn't it? For me to give it all up?"

"What would David and Chris say?"

"*They'll understand. They'll keep going. They'll do what needs to be done.*"

"*It's not that easy, Mike.*"

"*Of course it is. Why wouldn't it be?*"

"*Because you don't really mean it. It's just the dreams talking.*"

"*Stop saying that. It's not.*"

"*But it is,*" Mia said. "*You know it is. Just listen to yourself. The real you would never talk like that.*"

"*I've changed.*"

"*Men like you don't change so easily.*"

"*I don't understand why you're saying this. I thought you'd be happy.*"

"*Mike, I need you to wake up now.*"

"*What? Why?*"

"*Because if this dream continues, I'm going to die.*"

"*What? No!*"

"*You can't stop it, Mike.*"

Recker immediately started looking around frantically, searching for the first sign of trouble. There was none to be found though.

"*I can stop it. I can stop everything.*"

"*You're not superhuman, Mike. You can't save everyone. Not even me.*"

"*Stop talking like that.*"

"*You know why you keep having these dreams, don't you?*"

"*No, why?*"

"*Because you're afraid of losing me. You know, deep down inside, that as long as you do what you do, eventually one of us*" is going to be ripped away from the other. You know that's true."

"No, it's not."

Mia put her hand on Recker's face and smiled. "You know it is. Denying it isn't helping you. It's only prolonging your torture."

"I'm not going to lose you."

"Mike, it's already predetermined. My fate was sealed the moment you walked into my life. There's nothing you can do to prevent it."

"I can. I promise you that won't happen."

Mia sighed and shook her head, knowing how stubborn he could be. "You keep having these dreams because you know with each passing day, the odds are only increasing that one day, one of us won't be here any longer. We'll never grow old together. That's just not how it works for men like you. You go down in a blaze of glory, not in a nursing home."

"That's why I'm quitting."

"You'll never quit. It's just not in you. Everything's in your head right now. Your dreams are simply your fears for the future, what you know is likely to be true. You'll probably always have them. They're not going to stop anytime soon."

"I promise you that's not how we'll end up. It's not how you'll end up. I won't let that happen."

"It's too late, Mike. It's already begun."

"What has?"

Mia turned her head, looking back to the cafeteria entrance doors. Recker's eyes glanced over to them as well. They saw Haley walking in, followed closely by Jones.

Mia turned back to Recker and smiled. "There they are."

Recker looked confused. "Why are they here? I didn't tell them to come."

"You still don't get it, do you? It's just part of the dream."

As Haley and Jones approached the table, Recker and Mia stood up.

"What are you guys doing here?" Recker asked.

"We're here because of you," Jones replied.

"I don't understand. What's that mean?"

"It means you're done. You really thought you could just walk away from us and not have any consequences?"

"You guys can do the job without me," Recker said.

"Nobody walks away from us."

"Just listen to them, dear," Mia said, putting her hand on her boyfriend's face again.

"It's time to end this," Haley said.

"End what?"

"You need to come back to us without having all these other things to worry about."

Recker looked like he still didn't understand. Mia turned back around to face her friends. Haley pulled a gun and pointed it at her.

"I'm ready," Mia said.

"What?" Recker said. "What's going on?"

"This has to end," Haley said, holding his arm straighter, getting ready to fire.

Recker couldn't believe what was about to happen. "No, wait!"

Haley fired two times, both bullets entering Mia's midsection. Blood rolled down out of the corner of her mouth as she held her stomach. She smiled at Recker.

"I love you. But this is how it ends for us."

Mia slumped down to the ground as Recker looked on in horror. He looked at his friends, who were simply smiling at him, seemingly pleased with their despicable actions. Recker then flopped down to the ground and held Mia in his arms as the last breath of life faded out of her.

Recker sat up like he'd been shot out of a cannon, breathing as heavy as if he'd just run a marathon. He looked down at Mia's spot beside him and put his hand on her pillow. He then leaned back, letting his head rest against the wall behind him. He closed his eyes for a moment.

"It was just a dream," he whispered.

Recker looked at the clock and saw it was only two-thirty. He reached over to the end table and grabbed his phone. He scrolled down to Mia's number and was about to call her, just wanting to hear her voice for a minute or two, but then put his phone back. If he called for no reason, she was bound to know something was up, and would likely guess at the culprit. He didn't want her worrying about him while she was at the hospital. Instead, Recker slouched back down onto his back, then rolled onto his side as he contemplated whether he even wanted to try to fall back asleep again. At this point, he'd rather be tired than have to relive the same nightmares in his head over and over again.

Eventually, Recker did fall back asleep again, though it took him another hour to do so. He was planning on having breakfast waiting for Mia when she got in since she'd done it for him so many times, not that he planned on anything special, just bacon and eggs, but he was so tired, he slept through his alarm. He did wake up, though, at the sound of keys wiggling and the front door opening. Recker jumped out of bed and went into the living room, him and Mia locking eyes as soon as he appeared in the frame of the door. They both immediately went to each other and embraced, each of them happy to have the other in their arms.

"I was planning on having breakfast ready for you," Recker said. "I overslept a little bit."

"That's sweet of you, thank you."

"Just sit down and I'll make something for you."

"No, that's all right, really... I'm not really hungry."

"Are you sure? It's no trouble."

Mia kissed him on the lips. "Positive. Thank you for the offer, but I'm really just tired more than anything."

"How'd your night go?"

"Long. It was so busy, and we were already short-handed. It felt like everyone in the world had a baby in the last twenty-four hours. How about you? How was your night?"

"Fine."

"Manage all right without me?" Mia asked.

"It was a struggle."

"You look tired."

"I kept waking up. Probably because you weren't next to me."

Mia smiled, though she knew that wasn't the reason. She could guess what his issue was. "You had another one, didn't you?"

"I don't really wanna talk about it. I'm fine."

"Are you sure? It might do you good to get it out of your system."

"No, I'm fine. Really. You're tired anyway. The last thing you need right now is for me to throw some more of my issues on you."

"You know there's nothing else in the world that's more important to me than you are. Tired or not, I'm here."

"I know you are. But I want you to be selfish and take care of yourself for a change. We can always talk about it later."

"OK. What time do you have to leave?"

"Maybe an hour or so."

"You know what I would really like?" Mia asked.

"What's that?"

"For us to just lie down in bed and hold each other until you leave."

Recker smiled at her. "I think we could arrange that."

Recker and Mia went to their bedroom and snuggled each other underneath the sheets. As Recker held her, his mind went back to his dream, seeing her killed right in front of him. He closed his eyes, trying to shut it off, though it was no use. It kept replaying in his mind over and over again. Here he was holding this beautiful woman in his arms, and all he could think about was bad thoughts. He just wanted a positive image entering his mind for a change.

"You guys got anything interesting going on today?"

Mia said groggily, sounding like she was about to drift off to sleep.

"Uh, no, I don't think so. At least nothing I'm aware of. Never know how the day will unfold though."

There was silence for another minute, and though Recker wasn't a big small-talker, he actually preferred it in this instance if it helped to prevent him from what he was previously thinking.

"Hey, if I happen to fall asleep before you go, wake me up before you leave, OK?" Mia said.

"I'm not gonna wake you up. You need to sleep."

"Would you at least kiss me then?"

"There's nothing I would like better." There was silence for another minute. "You think you're gonna sleep the day away?"

There was no reply though. Recker tilted his head away and looked at his girlfriend's face, thinking she looked like an angel when she was sleeping. His thoughts then turned to what Mia said in his dream, about them being one day closer to one of them being ripped away from the other. He hoped this wouldn't be that day.

2

Recker got to the office, and as often as the case was, Jones and Haley were already there waiting for him. Recker didn't even try to beat them in anymore. It was a useless endeavor. He just wasn't making it there first, or even second on most days. Jones gave Recker a sharp eye when he walked in, then looked at his watch.

"It looks as though you've seen better days already," Jones said. "And it's only nine o'clock."

"You sleep at all?" Haley asked.

"I got a few minutes here and there," Recker answered.

"You've looked tired lately," Jones said. "You're not getting enough sleep."

"I'm fine."

"Perhaps, but, is there something troubling you that's preventing you from sleeping?"

"It's nothing. I'm just having one of those stretches

that everybody gets from time to time when they have trouble falling asleep."

Haley rubbed the stubble on his face, thinking back to a conversation he had with Mia about dreams. He wondered if he should bring it up, knowing he wasn't likely to get the truth anyway, and that it might rub his partner the wrong way. But Haley also thought that if he mentioned it, maybe Recker would know that he knew, and maybe it would be enough to springboard a conversation between the two of them about it. Haley also would have nightmares from time to time, and judging by Recker's appearance lately, and by Mia's conversation, that it was probably worse than anything he'd ever experienced. Haley suspected it was a daily, or at least fairly regular occurrence.

Haley suspected that every operative that had ever been overseas on multiple missions, who'd done some of the things they'd done, would have nightmares sometimes. He just figured it went along with the job. One of the perils of doing the work that they'd done... is that it never really leaves you. Even when it's finished. It always remained in the mind and in the soul. For him, Haley figured he had a bad nightmare about once a month. There didn't seem to be any trigger for it that he could tell. Sometimes it was after a case, sometimes it was in the middle of a dry spell, it didn't seem to matter. He couldn't figure out a cause. It just happened. And as he looked at Recker, there was a man who was carrying around a load with him. He didn't talk about it with Jones, and he wasn't sure if Jones noticed the same things he did, but he could see it on Recker's face, his

MIKE RYAN

body language, the way he stood, the way he moved, everything about him. It was a man who seemed tired. Tired of whatever images were flashing around in that head of his.

"Having bad nightmares or anything?" Haley asked, blurting it out.

Jones stopped typing and looked at Recker, wondering if maybe Haley had hit on something.

Recker didn't like being the center of attention and wanted to get this line of questioning over with so they could start their real business. His eyes glanced over between his two friends, without moving his head at all. "No, why?"

"Just asking. Thought maybe that's why you weren't sleeping."

Recker shook his head. "I'm good. Like I said, just one of those stretches. I'm sure I'll get back to normal soon."

"OK," Haley said, not wanting to press him too much on it. Recker was the type of man that the more you dug into him on something, the more he would draw away. That was the last thing anyone needed.

"Now that we're done with the couch and therapy session, maybe we can get back to work now?" Recker asked.

"Excellent idea," Jones said.

"Anything on the agenda?"

"If it happens as I think it will happen, we will probably have a situation come down later today."

"Why? What's up?"

"We picked up some texts and voicemails between

12

several individuals that I'm putting up on the big screen now."

Recker and Haley walked over to the fifty-inch monitor hanging on the wall, standing inches away from it as Jones started putting his information on it. Pictures of eight men appeared on the screen.

"Pleasant-looking bunch, aren't they?" Haley said.

"Pleasant indeed," Jones replied. "In this case, the looks match the men."

"Bad guys, I take it?" Recker asked.

"Bad doesn't even begin to describe them. This is as rough-and-tumble of a crew as we've ever come across."

Recker shot Jones a look. They'd handled some pretty bad dudes in their time. Saying this group might be the worst was either a bit of a stretch or it would be overly terrifying.

"We've dealt with some pretty bad hombres, David."

"Oh, I'm well aware, believe me. But this crew is a little different than the others we've come across."

"How so?" Haley asked.

"Because they just entirely rely on brute force. Unlike Nowak, Jeremiah, Vincent, or any of the other people we've come across, these guys don't try to outsmart you or make you think they're coming from a different direction. They're coming head on and they don't care if you know it. They're coming straight for you and they dare you to get in their way."

Recker and Haley continued to look at the names and faces on the screen to get familiar with them.

"How come I don't recognize any of these people?" Recker asked.

"Because they've only been here for a few weeks."

"Here? They've moved?"

"Oh, indeed they have," Jones answered.

"Where were they before?" Haley said.

"Mostly New Jersey and Delaware. That's where most of my information is coming from."

"What are they doing here?"

"Establishing a presence."

Recker shook his head as he looked at the screen. "When's it gonna end? Every time a challenger for Vincent's throne gets knocked off, there's a new one coming."

"Well, while I normally would understand the connection, you would be off base in this instance," Jones replied.

"What?"

"This group has no interest in taking over a city from underneath it."

"Then what do they want?"

"The short and easy answer is to take as much money and inflict as much brutality as they can before they move on."

"Why here?" Recker asked. "Why now?"

"As far as I can make out, it is police pressure driving them out. That was the reason they relocated from New Jersey to Delaware initially."

"So, the same thing will happen here."

Jones put his hand up, indicating that would not be as easy as it sounded. "In both cases it took over five years to drive them out. Now if it takes that much time here, then..."

"Then a lot of people are going to get hurt."

"A lot is putting it mildly. The estimates that I could get my hands on indicate that this gang is believed to be responsible for close to a hundred murders in the past ten years. And that's just the start of it. Hundreds of others have been put in the hospital at their hands."

"Who are their usual targets?"

"The best answer I can give you is just about anyone," Jones said. "Young, old, black, white, innocent, criminal, nothing much matters to this bunch. If you've got what they want, they will take it from you. And they will take no prisoners in doing so. They are violent and will use whatever means are at their disposal."

"Is it just these eight?" Haley asked.

Jones didn't immediately reply, causing both men to look back at him. With a sigh, Jones hit a button on his computer, and then looked up at the screen again.

"Hardly," Jones said.

The faces on Recker and Haley pretty much said it all. A look of surprise and horror encapsulated their expressions. They watched as the fairly large pictures of the eight men were replaced with the much smaller pictures of dozens more.

"Is this all of them?" Haley said.

"At least the ones that have been publicly identified," Jones replied. "Who knows how many more they've recruited that aren't known yet?"

"There must be close to a hundred people here," Recker said.

"No, not quite. Only eighty-three."

Recker's eyes almost bulged out of his head as he looked at the screen. "Only eighty-three," he whispered.

"Where are we gonna start?" Haley asked.

"I'm in the process of working on that now," Jones answered.

"They're already here?" Recker asked.

"Indeed, they are."

"For how long?"

"Earliest I can make out is they arrived sometime last week."

"And these are the guys you're saying we might have to deal with today?"

With a worrisome look in his eye, Jones went back to his computer screen. "Unfortunately."

"I'm hoping we're not going to deal with all eighty-three guys today," Recker said.

"I wish I could tell you how many there will be, but I can honestly say that I don't know. It could be three. It could be thirty."

"Wonderful. Just what is it they're going to be hitting today?"

"I'm still working on that," Jones replied.

Recker looked at the time. "Still working on it? When you gonna know?"

"When they say something definitive."

"But you know it's gonna be today?"

"That would be correct. Sometime around three o'clock."

"Well, do you have an area?" Recker asked.

Jones looked up at him. "I do not. I have a time. That's it."

"Just great."

Haley continued looking at the screen, amazed at the amount of people he was watching. "Not that I particularly care about the odds, or being on the short-end of the stick, but how are we gonna go up against eighty-three people?"

"Hopefully one at a time," Jones answered.

"As unlikely as that is," Recker said. "Chris is right. We're gonna need help."

"And just what did you have in mind?"

Recker gave him a grin. "There's only one man in this city that can help."

"Don't say it."

"You know who I'm talking about."

"Why don't we just put our offices next to his?" Jones sarcastically said. "We work with him so much we might as well be paying him rent."

"How organized is this bunch? Do they have a name or anything?"

"Well, they call themselves the Tri-State Scorpions."

Recker wasn't impressed. "Clever."

"As far as being organized, they do not have a de facto leader. They make decisions as a group. Exactly what that process is like or how involved it is I cannot say. It could be something like a general council or it could be everyone."

"So how do they determine what to hit then?"

"As I just explained to you, we don't know. Perhaps there's a ten-person board that approves everything. Perhaps everyone is free to do whatever they like within certain parameters. Perhaps it's some combination of the two. Right now, your guess is as good as mine."

"And how many of them are you tracking right now?"

"Right now, I've got three of their numbers."

"How'd you manage that?" Recker asked.

"Same way I always manage it. The system picked up on a couple of words within the covered radius and alerted me."

"Any idea what they're planning? I know you don't have an address yet, but is it a bank, convenience store, drugstore, anything?"

"Yes. Could be any of the above," Jones replied.

"Thanks. Very helpful."

"I'm giving you all the information I've got at the present time."

"Is it possible this thing could go down without us?"

"Extremely possible."

"Wonderful."

"Stop saying that."

"Is there anything you need us to do?" Recker asked. "Something to speed things along?"

"No, not a thing."

"In that case, I'm gonna make a phone call."

"Don't do it," Jones said.

"Got to."

Jones sighed, already knowing he had lost the battle. Recker was going to call Vincent for help again. He looked up from his computer only to see that Recker was already on the phone.

"Mike, what can I help you with?" Vincent asked.

"It's something urgent. Can we meet today?"

"Uh, yeah, I think I have room in my schedule. How's one o'clock sound?"

"I can make it," Recker said. "Where?"

"Let's make it the same place as usual. I missed breakfast today."

"I'll be there."

As Recker put his phone back in his pocket, he glanced over at Jones, who was sitting at his computer still shaking his head.

"A little more discussion would have been nice before getting us in bed with him again," Jones said.

"We're so far in bed with him at this point, what's the difference? Right now, I'll align myself with anybody to stop what I believe is the greater threat. And right now, it's those creeps on the screen."

3

Vincent and Malloy were already sitting down in the conference room of one of their delivery businesses, waiting for their visitors to arrive. The Tri-State Scorpions had already contacted Vincent via a third party to request a meeting, wanting to meet with the crime boss to announce their arrival in the city and surrounding area. Vincent was already well aware of the gang's reputation, and though he'd never formally met them before, both sides knew of the other.

"What did Recker want?" Malloy asked.

"Didn't say. Just said it was urgent."

"Wonder what that's about."

"Don't know," Vincent said. "Could be just about anything."

"What time?"

Vincent looked at his watch. "About two hours from now."

About five minutes later, one of Vincent's subordinates walked into the room to let them know that one of the Scorpions had arrived.

"He been frisked?" Malloy asked.

After getting the word that their visitor was clean, Vincent was eager to have the meeting begin. "Show them in."

"How you think this is gonna go?"

"We shall see."

The door then opened, Vincent's man stepping to the side to let Tommy Billings in. Billings was a fairly big man, standing over six-foot-three, and well over two hundred pounds, and could be an imposing sight with his bald head and goatee. Though Jones was right in that the Scorpions did not have a specific leader, in situations where someone needed to talk for the group, Billings was usually the man for the job. He could be an intimidating figure, he could talk the tough talk when it was needed, but he also was an intelligent guy and didn't succumb to making moves on impulse like many members of the group. While most of the Scorpions did opt for violence and brutality first, and Billings wasn't necessarily opposed to it when necessary, he also knew there were times when a softer touch was needed for the survival of the group. He knew, sometimes, diplomacy was the best option.

Vincent stood up to shake his visitor's hand. "Mr. Billings, pleasure to meet you."

"Likewise," Billings replied, reciprocating the handshake.

Vincent pointed to a chair. "Have a seat."

"Thank you."

Vincent then pointed to his most loyal soldier, seated by his side. "This is Jimmy Malloy."

"Ahh, the famous right-hand man of yours. I've heard of you as well."

"Nothing good I hope," Malloy said.

Billings grinned. "A mixture. Thought you'd be a little taller though."

"Now that the pleasantries are out of the way, what can I do for you?"

"As you may or may not be aware, we've been relocating our base of operations from Jersey the last few years."

"I'm well aware of your migration pattern."

"The heat's been coming down on us pretty good lately."

"And you think it will be easier for you here?"

"Listen, I know you run things around here and you're the top dog, and I totally understand and respect that. We're not looking to get into a war with you. We just want to peacefully coexist together."

Vincent smiled, thinking it was an odd choice of words. "I didn't think peaceful and Scorpions could coexist in the same sentence together."

Billings let out a small laugh. "Fair enough. I should tell you in all honesty, that some of the boys wanted to just roll into town and get rid of whoever gets in our way, you included."

"I should tell you that you wouldn't be the first to try.

There were the Italians, Jeremiah, Nowak, and a bunch of other small-timers. I'm still here. They're not."

"We might be a little more formidable than those people."

"Perhaps. Or maybe you would just occupy more space in the cemetery. Make no mistake, I was aware of your presence the minute you drove into town. You see, unlike your crew, war and violence is very seldom my first option or preference. But once I'm there, I will be as ruthless as anyone."

"I don't doubt that."

"You should also know that I operate in many circles. What you see isn't always what you get. And you don't always know where it's coming from."

"I've heard that," Billings said.

"I've got people employed in many different facets. Some work for me directly on a day-to-day basis, some work in financial sectors, some put on a blue suit and patrol around in a police car, some are detectives, some work in various other business interests, and I even have a few working for good old Uncle Sam. Believe me when I tell you, you don't want to make me for an enemy."

Billings nodded, knowing exactly how formidable of a threat Vincent was. Nothing he was hearing was new to him. The rumors of how far Vincent's hand stretched were known far and wide.

"And I believe that. Like I said, I didn't come here to threaten."

"Then what exactly do you want?" Vincent asked.

"Listen, we all know you're a powerful man. You've got

influence all over the place. No one disputes that. I think that if we wanted to take over, we'd have a hell of a fight. We're not some pushovers."

"No question about it."

"You'd have your hands full," Billings said. "Maybe you'd win, but it'd come at a high cost. Just the same, we might win, but it would also come at a high cost."

"Sometimes that's just the price of victory."

"It is. But it's not one we're interested in playing with right now. We're riding in holding the white peace flag so to speak."

"For what purpose?"

"Just for the purpose of coexisting, man. We know us riding in, you could take it as a threat and act out against it. That's not what we want. We also know that if we start hitting places that belong to you, that wouldn't be good either. We just wanna hang around, do our thing, and not have any beef with you."

"So, what, you want my blessing to have you here?"

"If you wanna call it a blessing, sure, I'd prefer to think of it as a truce. Neither side acts out against the other. There's plenty of room for the both of us without either side getting stupid about it. That's all I'm saying. We're not here to take over. Just doing our thing."

"That itself may present a bit of a problem," Vincent said. "You see, I have business interests all over this city, including the surrounding suburbs. Most of them are not widely known. I can't just have you blindly knocking over places that may belong to me."

"One of the reasons why I'm here. Just let us know

what areas to stay clear of, or what places belong to you, and we'll skip right over them."

Vincent briefly looked at Malloy as he contemplated his options. He then stared Billings in the eyes for a minute. "I'm sure you can also see the perils of me just telling you what belongs to me. That wouldn't exactly be in my best interests."

"I'm trying to be cooperative here."

"I'll tell you what I can do. I'll assign someone to be your contact. Whatever you plan on hitting, you clear it with him first. If it's mine, or something for reasons of my own that I don't want touched, you steer clear. If it's not, you have a green light."

"I don't know if the boys are gonna like having to get permission to do what they want."

"That's my best offer," Vincent sternly said. "You're free to take it or leave it."

"I'll have to take it back to the boys and discuss it with them first if you don't mind?"

"Take all the time you need. In the meantime, if something gets hit that belongs to me before you give me your answer, you might as well not come back with one. In the same vein, if you agree to these terms, and then choose to ignore them, or don't follow them to the letter, you'll be choosing your own fate. I hope I make myself clear."

"You absolutely do. I'll take it back to the boys." Billings got up and then reached his hand across the table to shake. "It was a pleasure to meet you, sir."

Vincent once again returned the handshake. "The pleasure was all mine." Billings turned around and was about to leave before Vincent spoke up again. "Oh, before you go, you should also know that I'm not the only main player in this town."

"Oh?" Billings said. "I was under the impression you had no other rivals."

"Not in this capacity, you're right, I don't. But there are other powerful people in this city who also will not take your arrival so happily."

"If you're talking about the law, we'll deal with them when the time comes."

"I'm talking about something much bigger than the law and a hundred times more lethal."

"And what would that be?"

"There's a man who works in the city called The Silencer," Vincent said.

"Yeah, I've heard of him."

"I should warn you that he is an incredible threat."

"I think we can deal with him."

"Others have said the same."

"We're not the others," Billings said. "We have over eighty members right now. I think we can deal with one man."

Vincent grinned. "As you wish. I just felt you should be adequately warned about the dangers."

"Appreciate it. So, who is this guy? I've heard some pretty wild stories about him. What is he, some kind of jacked-up superhero?"

"Well I don't know his real name or his backstory, but I've seen his work up close. As far as I'm concerned, there is no one better."

"Sounds like you got a deep affection for this guy."

"I would love to put him on my payroll. But he marches to his own drumbeat."

"So, you two aren't on the same side."

"The Silencer is on his own side."

"So how is it that you two coexist?"

"Because he and I made an agreement long ago not to interfere in each other's business, similar to the offer I made to you. So far, we've both kept our ends of that agreement. We stay out of each other's way. I'll say it again. I'll warn you to stay out of his."

"Thanks again."

Billings then turned around again to leave. Vincent and Malloy were quiet as they watched the man exit the room.

"Make sure he exits the facilities in the proper fashion," Vincent said.

Malloy got up and left the room, making sure that Billings left without any trouble. There was always the odd chance that the Scorpions were using the meeting as a cover to get Vincent into one spot so they could take their shot at taking him out in one swift stroke. Thankfully, there would be none of that on this day. Malloy returned to the conference room a few minutes later.

"He's gone," Malloy said. "No problems."

"No problems indeed."

Malloy sat down across from his boss to further discuss the meeting. "You don't really believe all that, do you?"

"You think he came in here and lied to my face?"

"Boss, you know their reputation as well as I do. They don't peacefully coexist with nobody. If they come in here, if we let them come in here, we're eventually gonna have to deal with them. And not by talking."

"What do you propose?"

"Let them know they're not welcome here. Don't even let them get a foothold."

"They have a large group," Vincent said. "It wouldn't be an easy endeavor. And after just recently getting rid of Nowak, I'm not sure we have the stomach to take up such a task at the moment."

"Even if we're not at full strength right now, we might not have any other choice."

"There is always another choice. If we decide to throw down against this group right now, it would be like two giant behemoths in the gladiator ring, just taking turns annihilating each other. It wouldn't be pretty. And it could decimate both sides."

"What's the alternative?"

"We wait. We plan. We keep an eye on them. We don't let our guard down. We make plans to put something in place for when they get out of line, then we're able to end it quickly without it turning into a bloodbath."

"OK. We can do that. How come you didn't tell him about both Silencers?"

"I think that's something that's best left for them to discover for themselves," Vincent replied. "And if there's one thing I know about Mr. Recker and friends, I'm sure they'll be knocking on their door soon enough."

4

For once, Recker had actually beaten Vincent to the diner. He knew it was probably only because it was a little later than their usual meetings and assumed that Vincent had gotten tied up with other matters. Not that Vincent was late, as it was still only ten minutes to one. But he knew Vincent also usually liked to arrive much earlier than this. While he waited, Recker sat down at their usual table and ordered something small.

Malloy was the first one in the door, getting there exactly at one o'clock. He and two other men went around the diner to make sure there were no obvious warning signs. Once they cleared the place, one of the men went out for their boss. Malloy went over to Recker as they awaited Vincent's arrival.

"A little late, huh?" Recker asked.

Malloy grinned. "Duty calls. And we're not late." Malloy looked at his watch. "We're right on time."

"I was under the impression that according to Vincent, if you're right on time, then you're late. Is that not so?"

Malloy continued smiling, always enjoying the back-and-forth with Recker. He then looked toward the door and saw Vincent coming in, so he walked over to him.

"He's already here, boss."

"Ah, good," Vincent said.

Malloy took his usual spot near the door so he could spot anyone coming in who wasn't exactly a friend to them. Vincent went down and took a seat across from Recker.

"I apologize for my lateness. I was tied up with some other business."

"Happens," Recker said.

Vincent noticed some appetizers on Recker's plate. "I see you ordered already."

"A little hungry."

Vincent grabbed a menu and ordered something himself. After putting the menu away, he inquired about the purposes of their meeting.

"So, you said this was urgent. What's on your mind?"

"The Tri-State Scorpions," Recker said. "What do you know about them?"

"I know they're a very dangerous group."

"Did you know they're now in the city?"

"I've heard something to that effect."

"Well I've heard that they're moving their base of operations from Delaware to here."

"That would be on point to what I've heard as well."

Recker could see by the lack of surprise or emotion on

Vincent's face, that this information wasn't new to him. It seemed a little odd that a man of his position wouldn't be worried about a new gang coming in, possibly going against him.

"You don't exactly seem concerned or anything."

"If we're being truthful here, I've already had a meeting with The Scorpions."

"You have?" Recker said, a little surprised himself.

"Not more than two hours ago."

"Don't tell me you're throwing in with them."

Vincent smirked. He didn't throw in with anybody unless it benefitted him somehow. And usually more than the other party. "No, they requested a meeting with me to let me know they weren't coming in with hostility."

"They wanna be friends?"

"Well, let's just say they don't want to be enemies at the moment."

"That's surprising," Recker said. "I was under the impression they didn't play nice with others."

"They don't. I'm well aware of The Scorpions reputation, their history, their methods. They're a group that bears watching."

"So, you accepted their peace terms?"

"Let's just say I made them an offer. I'm waiting to hear whether it's been accepted."

"Is there something about this that seems strange to you?"

"Such as?"

"They're known as a violent group that answers to no

one, will go up against anyone, takes and does what they want... but they're not doing that here?"

"I assume it's because they want to come in quietly and get their bearings straight before they get too hot and heavy."

"And you think you won't be one of their targets?" Recker asked.

"Mike, if you're asking me if I trust them and they'll live up to any truce agreements, then the answer is no. I don't trust them as far as I can spit."

"But you're letting them move in? That doesn't seem like it would be good for business."

"First of all, I've told them that if they don't want problems from me, then they'll leave my interests alone. They're free to hit anything that doesn't belong to me."

"And you think that'll satisfy them?"

"In the beginning."

"You know they'll keep wanting more," Recker said.

"I suspect as much."

"But you're still letting them in."

"Mike, there's still a lot of heat from what went down with Nowak. If I make a stand against The Scorpions now and get into another war, that's going to bring more heat than I'm prepared to deal with. Plus, I'm still operating shorthanded from that last business. The Scorpions are a powerful force. I'm not prepared for an all-out assault from them yet. This is the strategic option. I'll let them in. I'll keep a close eye. And I'll wait."

"For?"

"For the right opportunity. I'm well aware they're not

going to be satisfied with just doing what I tell them. Eventually they're going to want what I have. That's inevitable. If I go against them, run them out, it must be in the shadows to avoid a full conflict that would undoubtedly batter and bloody both sides. I can't allow my group to be decimated so soon after Nowak. It could cripple me and allow another force to come in and easily displace me."

"A lot of people are going to get hurt."

"Saving the city is your department. I did give them a warning about you though. They've already heard of your exploits."

"Oh?"

"They didn't seem impressed. I didn't tell them your name or anything about your partners, however. I'm sure they'll find that out soon enough on their own."

"So, you're not onboard with driving them out right now?"

"Not if it means my name gets attached to it," Vincent answered. "I can't afford for something to happen to them and have them think I'm involved somehow. If they think I'm behind it, another war is a certainty. And a war between me and The Scorpions will devastate this city. It will be fifty times worse than anything that happened with Nowak."

"You know anything about what they're planning?"

"Nothing specifically yet, no."

"I can't just let this group run roughshod all over the city until you're ready to put your plan into place."

"I understand. But for my own reasons, I cannot interfere at the moment. I'll give you whatever help I can in that regard, as long as it doesn't come back to me. But if there's any chance of my name getting stamped to it, I cannot get involved."

"If it's just me, it's gonna take a long time to eliminate this bunch."

"Oh, I don't know. Take out five at a time every night, you'll have the whole thing wrapped up in two weeks." Both men laughed at the preposterous statement. "In all seriousness, though The Scorpions don't have a true leader, and they operate by committee, the man who does most of the talking for them and therefore has the biggest influence, is a man named Tommy Billings."

"I think I saw that name."

"I believe him to be more reasonable than the rest. More calculating. He may be the man you want to target first. Take him out, perhaps the rest of the group spins its wheels for a while as they figure out the direction to go."

"Maybe I'll do that."

"Of course, on the flip side, maybe you'd want to save him for last, as he seems to be what keeps the group under control, for whatever that's worth, and if he's out of the picture, maybe they go hog wild and destroy everything in their path."

"Something to think about, I guess. Have you thought about what you'll do if this group decides not to play ball with you?"

"Then I'll have to engage before I'm ready to and live with the consequences. But until that point, I'll have to keep my cards close to the vest."

"I understand. I probably won't be able to afford to do the same though. I'll take them out as soon as possible."

"And I wish you all the luck in the world in that endeavor," Vincent said. "And as I've mentioned, any help you need, as long as it's done on the down-low, just ask."

"So, loaning me ten of your boys to engage in a shootout's off the table, huh?"

Vincent smiled. "For now."

"I've heard they might have something going down today at three o'clock."

Vincent looked at his watch. "Doesn't give you much time."

"You heard anything about that?"

"I have not."

"Billings didn't mention anything at your meeting?"

"He did not."

"What happens if they hit something today that belongs to you before they agree to your terms?" Recker asked.

"Then I guess I would have to make a statement and change my terms to something more favorable to myself."

The two men finished their meals, while also continuing to discuss The Scorpions. Neither man's position would change though. For Recker, they were an immediate threat that needed to be dealt with swiftly. For Vincent, he was going to do what he usually did. Watch. Wait. And then strike when the right opportunity arose.

5

After the meeting with Vincent, Recker went straight back to the office, hoping Jones had something more concrete about what The Scorpions were planning. He would be disappointed, though, after learning the situation was the same as when he left. They hadn't learned anything new. And time was growing short.

"You don't have anything?" Recker asked.

"Unfortunately, not," Jones replied. "I'm not a magician. I can only decipher what's communicated through the usual channels, email, text, phone, I'm not a mind reader. If they don't use those methods of communication to devise their plans, there's not much I can do to learn about it other than make some guesses."

Recker sighed. "Yeah, I know. Doesn't make it easier to swallow though. Especially if someone gets hurt because of these clowns."

"We're doing everything we can, Michael, you know that."

Instead of standing around, thinking of all the things that could go wrong, Recker decided to make a more productive use of his time. He sat at a computer and started reading everything he could about The Scorpions, wanting to learn as much about them as possible.

"What about their earliest jobs in those other places?" Recker asked. "Maybe there's some kind of connection there. Maybe they like to hit a certain kind of place first to announce their presence."

Jones turned to his partner and smiled. "It's a good thought."

By Jones' lack of urgency at the suggestion, Recker could tell it was no good. "You already looked into it, didn't you?"

"I did."

"And?"

"No connection to be made," Jones answered. "Their first jobs in Jersey as far as I can tell, at least the ones that made headlines, were some high-profile robberies. They announced their presence in Delaware with some home invasions."

"Connection in the targets?"

"There is not. I checked six ways to Sunday. They're either not dumb enough or not sloppy enough to target the same people when they arrive."

Recker then looked around the room, finally noticing that Haley wasn't there. "Hey, where's Chris?"

"He went out and started cruising around. If something went down and we got wind of it, he wanted to hopefully be closer to the action than sitting here."

"Not a bad idea," Recker said. "Sitting here could add another twenty minutes to the timeline."

"Assuming that he's actually in the area of whatever goes down, which the probabilities of such are probably not all that high."

"Well, at least there's that chance."

"I suppose that's all we're hoping for now," Jones said. "A chance."

"I guess that's all we got right now, isn't it?"

"For now. Unless your other friend has a change of heart or something."

"Vincent doesn't usually have a change of heart," Recker said. "He analyzes everything before he makes a decision and sticks with it. And besides, he didn't say he wouldn't help. He just said it couldn't be out in the open right now. He doesn't wanna risk another war already."

"Logically speaking, I guess I can understand that."

"So that means, right now, we're on our own."

"They must be using some kind of base for operations," Jones said. "I sincerely doubt that they're operating out of grandma's basement or some other rudimentary type of place."

Recker sat there for a minute, trying to clarify his own thoughts. "I think we're going about this wrong."

"How so?"

"Let's get ahead of them."

"I thought that's what we were trying to do?"

"No, we're trying to figure out where they're targeting

first. Whether we do or not, it's unlikely there's gonna be more than a handful of guys on that job, right?"

"Well, unless those plans involved knocking over ten banks at once or something."

"We need to stop them before they get started. Before they get a foothold, because once they do, getting rid of them is gonna be a whole lot harder."

"No complaints there, but how do you propose to do that?"

"Find one guy, tail him, let him take us to the rest."

"And how do you plan on finding that guy?" Jones asked.

"How about the texts you intercepted from those guys? Let's track them down."

"If it was that easy, Michael, I would have done so already. The fact that I didn't, or haven't, would suggest that those phone lines are no longer in operation or I can't pinpoint their location at the moment."

"What about Billings?"

"What about him?"

"We now know he's sort of a front-man for the group. We know he's met with Vincent, and is planning to do so again, maybe we can tail him."

"But we have no way to track him down to begin with," Jones replied. "I have no phone numbers related to him, no email addresses, no calls, no nothing. I do not have a starting point."

"We do. Vincent."

"You just said that Vincent is not going to give up anything if it will somehow get back to him. If you're suggesting that Vincent will let you stake out their next meeting, in the hopes of following Billings afterwards, then I think you need to have your head examined. He is not going to take the chance and allow that to happen. If Billings realizes he's being followed from that meeting, he's going to assume that Vincent set it up. Vincent knows that."

"Maybe. All we can do is ask."

Recker immediately took out his phone and made a call, hoping to get through to Vincent, though nobody answered right away. About ten minutes later, though, his call was returned.

"Mike, what can I do for you already?" Vincent asked.

"Had an idea, wanted to run it past you."

"OK, shoot."

"What if, whenever you have your next meeting with these guys, you let me know so I can tail them, find out where they're operating from?"

It didn't take Vincent long to think about it. Jones had him pegged right. "As much as I'd like to say yes, I'm afraid I can't. They know I wouldn't be careless enough to have someone tailing them from one of my meetings unless I put them up to it or allowed it."

"Yeah, David pretty much said the same thing."

"David's a smart man."

"Yeah, well, I won't tell him you said so. It was just a thought."

"Well, if you have any other thoughts that are more workable, let me know."

"I'll do that."

After Recker got off the phone, Jones could see that Vincent turned him down. Recker let out a sigh and had one of those faces he got when he wished things were going better for them.

"I guess it didn't go as well as you hoped," Jones said.

"Said the same thing you did."

"Well, I won't take any glee from being correct if that makes you feel any better."

"It doesn't."

"We'll find another way. We always do."

Recker aimlessly looked around before another thought popped into his head. "What if we tail Vincent on our own, without his permission?"

Jones' hands froze in midair as he was about to strike them down on the keyboard, shocked by the words that just came out of his friend's mouth. He then turned to the side, almost like he was a robot, and stared at him.

Recker noticed the strange look. "What?"

"Did I really just hear what I think I heard?"

"What?"

"Did you really just suggest that we tail Vincent?"

"Yeah. So?"

"And may I ask how well you think he would react to that if he found out?"

Recker shrugged. "We'll roll with it."

"Be that as it may, you know that's not as easy a task as it sounds."

"I know. He's got meeting places all over the city. He could choose any one of fifty places to meet with them."

"And probably fifty more that we don't even know about."

"What if we ping his phone?" Recker asked.

"We've been over that before. He knows we can track people that way, or at least heavily suspects it. Do you really think he's going to allow us to do that in this instance? I'm sure the phone he talks to you on isn't the only one he has, and it isn't always on. One of the issues with doing business with people you might eventually have to go against... they know your tricks."

The pair kept looking at the time, doing a sort of countdown, waiting until it got to three o'clock. They kept hoping that they'd hear something ahead of time, but it never materialized. Now, it was almost like they were at a wake. They were just waiting to hear what the damage was. Right at three o'clock, Haley called in.

"You guys hear anything yet?" Haley asked.

"That would be a negative," Jones answered.

"Whatever they were planning, maybe it got pushed back or canceled. Could be that's why we didn't hear anything else."

"I suppose it's possible."

Recker was not as convinced. "I don't think pushing back or cancelling are in these guy's vocabulary. I'm pretty sure whatever they plan, they stick to it, no matter what."

"Well if that's the case, we should be hearing word pretty soon," Jones said.

Recker looked at his computer screen, sad that they weren't able to figure out their plans. "Hopefully, they kept the destruction to a minimum."

6

Haley had long since returned from his outing and had taken a seat on the couch, just sitting there with his hands between his knees, waiting for word of some carnage that he wasn't even sure was coming. It was just assumed. Recker was basically doing the same thing, though he was on the computer. He wasn't doing much, though, basically just striking a couple keys every now and then just to pass the time.

Jones was the only one who was really avoiding the doldrums of believing they missed out on something. He was checking all his usual sources, newspapers, TV, radio, online blogs, websites, everything he could to determine what, if anything, went down at three o'clock. It'd been two hours now, and they still hadn't heard anything. That would soon change, though, as Jones suddenly sat up straighter and leaned forward, getting a better look at his screen. His change in demeanor wasn't lost on his friends, who noticed him acting differently.

"What?" Recker asked. "You find something?"

Haley got up and walked over to Jones' chair. "The Scorpions?"

"I don't know," Jones answered. "It could be."

"Well what is it?" Recker said.

Jones read off the screen, though he wished he didn't have to. His low-key voice, which had a tint of sadness in it, gave a clue to his partners as to what his message contained.

"Approximately two hours ago, a small mom-and-pop convenience store was robbed by what authorities believe to be three men. The husband and wife, Antonio Govindo, and his wife, Rosetta, both sixty-five, were killed in the robbery, though authorities believe they did not resist and were killed unnecessarily. Law enforcement officials say security cameras confirm that the store owners seemed to comply with the robbers, who were wearing masks and cannot be identified at this time. The robbers shot the husband and wife just before fleeing the store. The amount of money is yet to be confirmed, but unofficial sources say the till did not contain more than a hundred dollars. This is a developing story and we will keep you updated as we learn more."

After finishing reading, Jones just leaned back in his chair and stared at the screen. Haley went back to his couch and sat down. Recker put his elbows on the desk and put his hands on his head. Though there was nothing else any of them could have done, they each felt a bit responsible for the incident. Two innocent people were killed because they weren't able to find out where the robbery was going to take place. They knew something like this would happen. Innocent people being shot and killed for no reason other than The Scorpions to announce their presence or because they felt like it.

"A hundred dollars," Recker blurted out. "They were killed over a hundred dollars."

"I think the money was immaterial," Jones somberly said. "They didn't resist. Whether it was five dollars or a thousand dollars, the result would have been the same."

"David's right," Haley said. "They just wanted to kill someone. I bet they didn't even care about the money."

"They're announcing their arrival," Recker said.

"They wore masks," Jones replied. "Tough to announce your presence when nobody knows who you are."

"We know. And that's enough for me."

"What are we gonna do?" Haley asked.

"We gotta find these scumbags and find them fast," Recker answered. "Because if we don't, Mr. and Mrs. Govindo won't be the only innocent people getting buried."

"What about Tyrell? Maybe he can find out something."

"Tyrell's been resting since getting shot," Jones said. "Let's not push him back into the field before he's ready."

"It's all hands on deck right now, David," Recker said. "Chris is right. We need eyes and ears on the street and there's nobody better at that than Tyrell. He's gotta get back out there."

"Very well."

Recker immediately grabbed his phone and called Tyrell. The last time they spoke was a week ago, and Tyrell had said something about going down the Jersey shore for a little vacation. Hopefully, he was back as Recker would have hated to spoil his plans. But this was an urgent situation. Tyrell picked up on the second ring.

"Hey, what's up, buddy?"

"Hey," Recker replied. "Hope I'm not interrupting your vacation or nothing."

"Nah, just got back yesterday, actually."

"Have a good time?"

"Pfft, man, I feel great," Tyrell replied. "Almost feel like a new man. I can't tell you the last time I was down the shore. Sand, ocean, good-looking women, the salty air, almost feels like I was never shot."

"Glad to hear it. So, you're back in town then?"

"Yeah, like I said, got back yesterday."

"Good. I need you."

"What?"

"I need you."

"Awe, c'mon, man, I just got back."

"Well, you said you feel great," Recker said. "You feel like a new man."

"That was a minute ago. You can't even let me catch a breath or something?"

"You just had a week. Did I bother you?"

"Well, no."

"See? So now you're back and it's time to get back to work."

"Jeez, man, ever hear of working your way back in slowly?"

"Not really."

"Somehow, in your case, that don't really surprise me. You do everything full-throttle, don't you?"

"I try."

"I'm gonna need you and everyone you can round up," Recker said.

Tyrell loudly sighed into the phone. "This ain't gonna be an easy assignment, is it?"

"Not likely."

Tyrell sighed again. "What is it with you, huh? You just love to find trouble, don't you?"

"I look for trouble so it doesn't find others."

"Yeah, yeah, I know the spiel. So, what is it this time?"

"You know The Scorpions?"

"Can you hear yourself? Do I know The Scorpions? Man, I know everyone up and down the east coast. Of course I know The Scorpions. And I take it you know them now too. So, before you get started, let me give you some advice, they're about as ruthless and evil of a group as you can go up against. So, if you're thinking about doing something with them, turn that light bulb off in your head and just forget about it and stick to what's going down in this city, OK?"

"Can't."

"Why not?"

"They're already in the city," Recker answered.

"Oh, man, are you for real?"

"As real as it gets."

"Those jokers are here?"

"Rolled in some time in the past week as far as we can tell."

"Does Vincent know about this?"

"He does. He's working on some kind of truce for now."

"I would seriously suggest you do the same."

"Can't."

"Why?"

"Because they just killed two people today."

"Please tell me they were some lowlifes?"

"Two people in their sixties that were just operating their store," Recker replied.

"This ain't gonna be pretty."

"Nothing in this business ever is."

"I mean, these guys don't play around, man."

"Neither do I."

"Last I heard, they got like sixty men with them."

"We count over eighty."

Tyrell made some noises into the phone like he was going to cry. "You're really gonna do this to me, aren't you?"

"If you know their reputation, you know why we gotta end this before they get too settled. They've already killed two people. You know there will be hundreds more if we don't stop them."

"You do know we are not an army, right?"

"Ever hear of an army of one?" Recker asked.

"Yeah, but as badass as you are, and Chris too, unless you two can start cloning yourselves, you're seriously outnumbered. You won't live long enough to finish this fight."

"Let us worry about that."

"Your only chance of getting rid of these guys is getting Vincent on board."

"Well he's not, right now. So, we gotta get it started ourselves. What's the matter, you too afraid?"

"Hell, yes, I'm afraid. And if you had any sense in that head of yours, you would be too! This isn't some local gang or upstart organization biting off more than they can chew. These are some badass mofos."

Recker could hear the concern in his friend's voice, but no matter what he was saying, he knew Tyrell wouldn't turn him down. He didn't want animals like The Scorpions in town any more than Recker did. Tyrell was just more hesitant in getting started. He just needed that extra push that Recker so often provided.

"So, when can you get started?" Recker asked.

"Did you just hear everything that I said?"

"I did."

"Well then you heard me say that I don't want nothing to do with those guys. I just got healed up from being shot. I really don't want to make it a habit. And those guys won't have any problem in doing that, you know."

"I know."

"So, there you have it."

"So, can you start on it tomorrow?"

Tyrell let out a low-pitched grunt. "You're impossible, you know that?"

"So, I've been told. C'mon, Tyrell, you really want these guys in a city that you live in, that your brother lives in, your mother..."

"What are you gonna do, run down my entire family?"

"If necessary."

"Well, forget it, all right, just forget it."

"Tomorrow?" Recker asked again.

"Yeah, yeah, tomorrow, just stop talking."

"OK. I'll call you in the morning with some details."

"Yeah, yeah, can't wait. Goodbye."

Recker laughed as he put the phone down.

Jones looked at him as he waited for word. "Well?"

"He's in," Recker replied. "Told you he was fine."

"Sounded like you needed to do a little convincing."

"No more than usual."

"So, what do we do now, sit around and wait?" Haley asked.

"You know that's not usually my style."

"What else can we do? Unless David picks up another job, or Tyrell reports back with something, but that could take a few days at least, so what other options are there?"

Recker sat, thinking. He could think of one. As usual, it probably wouldn't go over well with Jones. But it was an option. As Recker sat there, silently deliberating, figuring things out in his own mind, Jones periodically looked over at him, and could tell he had something going on in that brain of his. Whatever it was, Jones was sure he wouldn't like it. Recker always got a certain look about him when he was thinking of something that seemed a little farther, a little deeper, than Jones thought they should go. This looked like one of those times. After several minutes of silence, Jones couldn't take the quiet sounds of just his fingers hitting the keyboard and knew Recker was thinking of something. He needed to know what it was.

Jones turned his chair to face Recker. "Will you just please spit it out?"

Recker snapped out of his stare. "What? Spit what out?"

"Whatever dangerous and mind-boggling plan you have going on in that head of yours?"

"What makes you think there is one?"

Jones gave him a stern look. "Really? I think I know you well enough by now to know that you've got something hatching up there."

Recker grinned. "I hate being predictable."

"So, what is it? Just say it and get it over with."

"Why do you always assume it's going to be bad?"

"Because it's you," Jones answered. "Whenever you come up with a plan, it is almost always not the safest way to go. On the contrary, it usually always involves us moving faster than we should and is probably the most dangerous thing we can do."

"It is not."

"Please, don't even try to argue that one."

"Well... OK, I guess you got me there."

"So, what is it?"

"In order to speed things up..."

"See?" Jones said. "I told you. You're always in favor of moving up the timeline."

"I'm in favor of trying to make sure innocent people don't get hurt or killed."

"Continue."

"Anyway, in order to get to them faster, what's the best way to do it?"

"Try and meet them head on," Haley replied.

"Right."

"Please, don't encourage him," Jones said.

"Let's set up a meeting with them," Recker said. "Let's lay all our cards on the table."

"You want to do what?"

"Set up a meeting."

"You actually want to meet with these people?" Jones asked, hardly believing it.

"Yeah, why not?"

"What makes you think you'll be alive at the end of it?"

"Well, we'll obviously have to take some precautions."

"Like, by not going?"

"No, there would have to be some stipulations involved," Recker said.

"I do believe you have finally flipped your lid."

"Makes sense," Haley said.

"Oh, no," Jones said, putting his head down on the table, knowing he was about to be outvoted again. It happened often.

"Think about it. If Mike meets with this Billings guy, I can go along too. They wouldn't be expecting me. I can either tail him, following the meeting, or I can put some tracking device on his car, and we can find out where he's going."

Recker pointed at his partner, liking the idea more and more. "Right. Let's be proactive about it."

"I see a whole host of problems with this," Jones said.

"Like what?"

"Well, you're saying to bring backup to follow him. What if they have the same thought and do the same to you?"

"I can lose a tail. I'm not even worried about that."

"But what if you bring backup, they bring backup, everyone sees each other, then a war breaks out right then and there."

"It's gotta happen, eventually."

"Yes, but hopefully that eventually will happen on our terms, when we want it to, and not have it sprung upon us."

"I can scout the area out ahead of time," Haley said. "If I notice activity I don't think I can handle, I could always back off."

Recker nodded, appearing to be pleased. Jones sighed, knowing he could throw out a hundred different scenarios for how this meeting could go sideways, but he knew his friends would have a rebuttal for every one of them. They always did. That was the main problem for Jones once they brought Haley on. Not that he ever regretted it, on the contrary, he felt it was the best thing they ever did. Haley was a good partner, and a good friend. Jones couldn't imagine doing the work without him again. But if there was one downside, it was bringing in someone like

Haley, who had similar experiences to Recker, and also similar thought processes. It was just how they were wired, partly from all the work they did in their previous work. But that also meant that whenever there was a difference of opinion, Jones was likely going to be outvoted. At least when it was just the two of them, Jones could every now and then win a debate. Now, it was almost impossible. The two former CIA agents almost always stuck together on any topic. But considering how valuable Haley was, and now seeming indispensable, Jones supposed it was a good tradeoff, even though it meant he usually didn't get his way.

Knowing he was defeated, Jones still had questions. "Considering we don't know where they are, exactly how do you plan on setting up this meeting?"

"That part's actually easy," Recker replied.

"Oh, really?"

"Yeah. Vincent told me he's waiting to hear back about the offer he made them. I'll call him, let him know what I want, that way when he hears back from Billings, Vincent can see if he's interested in meeting me. We'll see if he can arrange it."

"And did it ever occur to you that Vincent's letting these people stay in town because he sees more value in them than you?"

Recker looked at his partner strangely. "What, you think Vincent might set me up and let The Scorpions take me out?"

"Let's be honest here, Mike. Vincent's been a good ally for us, and us to them, for a long time now. But make no bones about it, Vincent will do what's best for Vincent. Always. And if the time comes when he feels there's someone out there that will help him in a better manner than you, don't think for a second that he doesn't view you as expendable."

"Maybe."

"And have you considered the possibility that maybe Vincent is letting them stay with the intention of eventually recruiting them into his own organization, thereby giving him almost untouchable status with any other rival that ever comes in? Nobody who's sane would ever think about going up against him again with The Scorpions in his back pocket. That would mean no more Nowak's, no more Jeremiah's, no more Italians, no more contenders to his throne. Ever."

"I guess in some way that makes sense. But I don't think that's what's happening here."

"I hope you're right. Because your belief and trust in Vincent could eventually come back to haunt you."

7

While Recker didn't put as much stock into Jones' theory as David did, Recker couldn't say it was completely without merit. He honestly did not believe that was what was happening, though he couldn't outright say it was impossible either. He just didn't think that was what Vincent was planning. At least not now. Recker would take him at his word that Vincent wanted The Scorpions out of town just as much. He just had a different way of going about it. Recker grabbed his phone to make the call. Before his fingers started pushing buttons, he glanced over at Jones, who he could feel was shooting lasers out of his eyes at him.

"You're really going to do this?" Jones asked.

"I think it's the best way."

"OK. Do what you think is best."

Recker knew that was Jones-speak for admitting

defeat, though he still wasn't backing off of his position. Nevertheless, Recker made the call. This time, he got right through to Vincent.

"Mike, nice to hear from you again. If we keep talking to each other at this rate, we might have to move in together."

Recker let out a laugh, though he really didn't think it was that funny. "Maybe so. Anyway, the reason I called is that I have another proposition for you."

"I appreciate your insistence, Mike, but my stance hasn't really changed."

"I'm not asking you to. I have something else in mind."

"Which is?"

"You're expecting to hear back from Billings at some point, right?"

"That's correct."

"Whenever that happens, I'd like for you to ask him if he'd be willing to meet with me."

Vincent was a little stunned at the request. It definitely wasn't something he was prepared to hear. "You want a meet?"

"That's right."

"Can I ask what you think the point of that would be?"

"I want him to know I'm coming," Recker replied.

"I have a feeling he already knows that."

"Listen, I know, for your own reasons, you wanna wait a while before making a move on them, and that's fine, you do what you gotta do. But I don't have the same stance."

"I understand that."

"Did you hear about a job that was pulled a few hours ago? A convenience store in the northeast, a man and wife in their sixties were killed."

"I heard something to that effect."

"I think they did it."

"I was under the impression the police had not identified anyone yet," Vincent said.

"I have my own reasons for believing it was them."

"And if it was?"

"Those people they killed were not a threat. I'm not gonna just sit around for months and watch innocent people get murdered because this group feels like it's fun and games."

"I can understand your feelings, Mike, I really can. But even if I set this meeting up for you, what would it accomplish? They're not going to stop, whether they know you're coming or not. And I don't see what good it would do for you to have them be ready for you. As good as you and Chris are, stealth is your only play here. You need to bob and weave, move in and out, going toe to toe with these jokers is not the wisest of moves. There's just too many for you guys to deal with at one time."

"I agree," Recker said. "That's why I don't plan to. We're gonna move in a way that makes sense. But I need that meeting first."

"You have something up your sleeve already, don't you?"

"I don't think it would do either of us any good if I answered that."

"I'll assume that's a yes."

"So, can you set it up?"

"It sounds like your mind is pretty much made up on this."

"It is."

"Where and when?"

"I need a place where I can be confident that Billings isn't going to have backup and end the meeting prematurely."

"Why do I get the feeling this still involves me?" Vincent asked.

"Maybe we could use one of your facilities. Your boys run security so neither of us can bring in any weapons and keeps out any surprise guests."

"An interesting proposition."

"I thought so. So, what about it? You think you can do it?"

Vincent hesitated for a second before answering. "Well, it may take a few days. I'm not sure when Billings is going to get back to me on my offer."

"That's fine."

"But when he does, I'll mention it and let you know what he says."

"That's all I can ask."

It was two more days before Vincent and Billings hooked up again. Instead of a phone call, they agreed to meet at the same place they did before. It was the same situation,

Vincent and Malloy waiting in the conference room, waiting for Billings to be led in after being frisked. Once he was in, Billings smiled at seeing the two men sitting next to each other again.

"You two come as a matching set?"

Vincent grinned, though he really didn't find it all that amusing. "In my position, I find it advantageous to usually have someone by my side during any external meeting. It has a tendency to relax things in the event the discussions get heated."

"Certainly understandable."

"So, your group has come to a decision?"

"We have," Billings answered. "We'll agree to your terms for now."

"For now?"

"Well, if we play by your rules for a while, and you see that we're willing to be flexible and work with you, maybe you'll relax those rules a bit later on."

"I suppose that could be arranged if the situation warrants it."

"Then it sounds like we got a deal."

The two men then got up out of their seats and shook hands to consummate their agreement.

"I do have some other things to discuss with you, however," Vincent said.

"Oh, yeah?"

"First off, I've heard you've already been busy. That hardly seems like the behavior of a friendly business partner."

"What are you talking about?"

Vincent looked to Malloy, who pulled out a newspaper article out of his jacket and handed it to him. Vincent briefly looked at it, then slid it across the table for Billings to see. Billings picked it up and read about the misfortunes of Antonio and Rosetta Govindo. He didn't bother to read the whole thing though. He was already familiar with the contents of the article. He lifted his eyes up and looked over the article at Vincent.

"If you're thinking this was our handiwork, it's not. This wasn't us."

Vincent and Malloy looked at each other, a little surprised that he was denying it. They assumed he would come clean as soon as they presented it to him. Unless he was telling the truth, which would have been an even bigger shock. That would have meant that Recker was wrong in accusing The Scorpions of the hit. They couldn't remember Recker ever being wrong before in anything. Anytime he ever thought someone was involved in something, they were. They knew he didn't go throwing accusations around lightly. If Recker said it was them, Vincent took it as gospel.

"So. you know nothing about this?" Vincent asked.

"I do not."

Vincent looked away for a moment, trying to articulate his words so that he didn't come across like he was calling the man a liar to his face, but also being stern enough in letting him know that he didn't believe him.

"I have it on good authority it was your group that was responsible."

"Whose authority is that?" Billings asked.

"Well, I'm sure you can understand that I can't reveal my sources."

"Some of those contacts in the police department, maybe?"

"Perhaps."

Billings coughed as he tried to think of a response. "Well, I can only speak to my direct knowledge of the situation, which is I don't know who's responsible for that. Maybe it was a couple of the guys acting on their own, which they've always been able to do freely."

"Do you have control of these people or not?"

"Well, I think it's important to note that, if this was us, it was done before we came to any sort of agreement with you. It wasn't your building, was it?"

"It was not. That doesn't really matter though if you're unable to reel your guys in."

"Nobody needs to be reeled in. I guarantee from here on out that we'll live up to our end of the agreement."

"I would hope so. I would hate for our arrangement to come crashing down so soon."

"As would I. Well if that's all, I'm sure we all have other things we need to attend to."

Vincent wasn't finished yet though. "Just a minute. We do have one other thing we need to discuss."

"Oh? Someone else get knocked over?"

"Not quite. I've received a request from someone to have a meeting with you. He asked me to pass it along."

"Getting famous already, huh?" Billings said with a smile. "Who's that?"

"The Silencer."

Billings' smile slowly faded from his face as the news sank in. "The Silencer wants to meet with me?"

"That would be correct."

"What for?"

"He didn't say."

"Talk with him often, do you?"

"The request was made through a familiar third party," Vincent replied. "The request was made and passed to me, and I'm passing it along to you."

"What's he wanna meet with me for?"

"That... I have no idea."

Billings then laughed. "Yeah, sure, I'll meet up with the crumb. Where and when? I'll bring the boys along and we'll end the guy for sure."

Vincent grinned. Obviously, the man had no idea how Recker worked. It was a situation of a man hearing the reputation, and thinking he knew all there was to know, but clearly didn't have a clue.

"It won't be quite so easy in that regard," Vincent said. "The request I received was for the meeting to take place here at a time that's convenient for you. It was suggested that I sit in to moderate and make sure neither party tried anything funny."

"What?"

"The Silencer is a very careful and intelligent man. You won't fool him. He's asked for both you and him to meet here, no backup, no weapons, with me here to screen both parties beforehand."

"Why you?"

"Probably because we have a mutual respect. He

knows I won't doublecross him. If this meeting is agreed to, then both parties will live up to the terms."

"All right, I can dig it. I'll meet with him."

"You agree to the terms?"

"Absolutely," Billings said. "Bring him on."

8

—————

Recker and Haley were getting ready to leave the office for their meeting. They each packed their bag with weapons, not that they were expecting to use most, if any of them, but just in case, they'd be ready. They figured they could trust Vincent. But The Scorpions were another matter. As they packed everything up and were ready to go, Recker made sure Jones was ready.

"You good?" Recker asked.

"I am ready. You're sure you wanna go through with this?"

"Why wouldn't I be?"

"Just making sure this is what you want."

"Stop worrying. It'll be fine. It'll work."

"I sure hope so."

"We'll call you when we're there."

Recker and Haley left the office and hopped in their separate cars to go down to the meeting place. The plan was for Haley to get there first, parking a long way away and walking the rest of the way so he'd avoid eyes or cameras. He had a tracking device on him that he was planning on planting somewhere on Billings' car. He wanted to be in place by the time Recker rolled up, that way nobody would think they were there together. Mostly in case The Scorpions were planning the same thing, or something similar. If the situation turned out that Haley couldn't get to Billings' car, whether there were people around, or other obstacles, he'd retreat back to his car and drive to a nearby spot where he could follow Billings coming out of the meeting. Then he could plant the tracking device on the car at a later time.

Recker and Haley got to the area at the same time, but Recker drove around for a while until his partner said he was ready. It would also give Recker a chance to see if he could spot anyone else who might have been lingering around. If so, it would likely be The Scorpions. But Recker drove around for over thirty minutes, without seeing any obvious signs of trouble awaiting.

"I'm not seeing anything," Recker said. "I'm gonna head in."

"All right," Haley replied. "I'm already on the move."

"Just remember you don't need to take chances. If you can't get close to the car, we'll go to Plan B."

"Right."

Recker then drove to the meeting place, going through a gate that had Vincent's men stationed on it. He didn't even have to be vetted anymore since all of Vincent's men were so familiar with him these days. He drove up to the main building and got out of his car to head inside. Once he went up the concrete steps and walked in the building, he was immediately greeted by ten more of Vincent's men. They started approaching him, but Recker already knew the deal. He reached inside his jacket and removed his gun, holding it out for one of the men to take it.

"Other guy here yet?" Recker asked.

"Not yet," Vincent's man replied.

Recker reached around to his back and removed his backup weapon and handed that over as well.

"That it?"

"Yep," Recker answered. He put his arms up and turned around so the men could frisk him.

They did a half-hearted job, knowing they weren't going to find anything else. They knew Recker well enough by now to know that he didn't try any tricks. He was as straightforward as they came. If he had a gun, he'd tell you, and if he didn't want to give it up, he wouldn't. One of the men led Recker into the conference room, where Vincent and Malloy were already waiting. Recker looked around to make sure that his opponent really wasn't there. Recker walked over to the table and shook hands with the two men. Vincent could tell by Recker's face that he was ready for this to begin.

"He should be here shortly," Vincent said.

"I can wait."

"You look like a man who has something to say."

"I do," Recker said.

"You really think this is going to accomplish something?"

"Wouldn't do it if I didn't."

"You know, he didn't admit to that mom-and-pop store robbery," Vincent said.

"You really expect him to?"

Vincent grinned. "No. I highly suspect that you're correct though."

As they continued talking, a minute later Malloy's phone rang. He answered it, though the conversation only lasted about ten seconds.

"He's here," Malloy said. "They're showing him in now."

Vincent and Malloy took a seat at opposite ends of the long rectangular table, as Recker took a seat in the middle, ready to go face to face with his new adversary. Another minute went by, then the door opened, Billings standing there. He looked at each of the men in the room, before his eyes finally settled on Recker. He didn't take his eyes off the man as he sat down across from him.

"I guess you must be the famous Silencer."

"Guess so."

"From your reputation I figured you'd be a little taller."

"From your reputation I figured you'd be a little wider."

Billings laughed. "Funny. I like a man with a sense of humor."

"Well, now that you two have been introduced, the rules of the road are that this will be a civilized meeting," Vincent said. "There will be no physical altercations or shouting. Jimmy and I are here in no capacity other than to observe and make sure both parties follow the letter of the deal that was arranged. We will not interfere or interject in any way unless it's to bring the discussion back to an acceptable level if it should get out of hand. Agreed?"

"Yep," Recker said.

"Agreed," Billings replied.

"With that being said, have at it," Vincent said.

"So, what'd you wanna talk about?" Billings asked.

"I know you guys pulled that job that killed the Govindo's," Recker replied.

"Don't know what you're talking about."

"Lying to me doesn't change the fact that I know you did it."

"And if we did, what's it to you?"

"I got a problem with it."

"What's your deal, man? You run around all over the place, trying to protect little old ladies from crossing the street, things like that. You got some superhero complex or something? Maybe you need some tights and spandex."

"The only thing I'm trying to do is get rid of scumbags like you."

"You talk a big game."

"And I back it up."

"You got something to say or not? I didn't come here just to hear you go on and on."

"Yeah, I got something to say," Recker said. "I'm gonna make you an offer."

"Can't wait to hear it."

"If you leave now, move on to a new city, I'll forget about what happened and let it go."

Billings smiled, appreciating the audacity of the man. "Oh, you will, huh? And if we don't?"

"Then I'm gonna kill every single one of you."

Vincent and Malloy looked at both men, the tension ramping up quickly. They thought it might get to this point by the end, but they didn't anticipate almost leading off with it.

Billings laughed. "You can't be serious."

"I don't make threats I can't back up."

"You know, I'm almost inclined to stick around just to see how you go about accomplishing this."

"You don't want me for an enemy."

"I could say the same for us. As far as I can see, you're just one man."

"So was Rambo."

Billings laughed again. He then briefly looked at Vincent and Malloy. "I love this guy. I really do. Dude, I would really hate to kill you when the time comes, I really would."

"Can't say the same about you."

As they were talking, Haley was on the perimeter of the property, trying to find a way to get to Billings' car. It was parked in front of the building, and there must have been ten of Vincent's men either around it or walking around nearby. There was no way he was going to be able to get to it without anyone knowing. Not unless he created some kind of diversion. And the only thing he could think of that would work would be to throw a bomb in the other direction to get everyone's attention. That was obviously going to an extreme that he couldn't and wouldn't go to.

With not knowing how long the meeting was going to last, Haley quickly made the decision to abandon Plan A. He scurried back to his car so he could move to a different position where he could follow Billings on the way out. He called Jones to let him know.

"David, I can't plant the tracker right now. Too many people around."

"So, what do you plan to do now?" Jones asked.

"Just like we said. I guess I'll follow him when he comes out. Wait for a better opportunity."

"Just make sure you're careful. He may be on the lookout for something like that."

"I will. I'm pretty sure I'm better at this sort of thing than he is."

"Just don't take him for granted. He's still dangerous."

"Will do."

Recker and Billings were continuing to throw threats around at each other.

"How about I make you an offer?" Billings asked. "How about you leave the city, and I'll make sure you don't get killed? How about that?"

"I'll pass."

"You're unbelievable, man, you know that? You got some gall. You realize who you're talking to?"

"Sure do."

"We got over eighty card-carrying members, man. What are you, one man? You really think you can stand up to us? You want a war with us, and we will squash you like a bug."

"Maybe. I just wanted to let you know, that if you stay,

and members of your group start dropping like flies, you'd know who was responsible for it."

Billings smiled. "You're unbelievable. I know you got some fancy reputation for taking care of people, and maybe it's deserved, I don't know. But I guarantee you that you have never gone against someone like us before."

"Well then it should be gratifying when the last of you are put underground. Because make no mistake, I'm not coming to put you in jail, or drive you away, or make you look bad in the court of public opinion. I'm coming to bury you."

"I'll make sure they put that on your tombstone. Here lies the man who bit off more than he could chew by messing with The Scorpions."

"I think I've said all I wanted to say," Recker said. "I believe we understand each other."

"We do."

"We'll be seeing each other again very soon."

"Can't wait." Billings then looked over to Vincent. "You got a hand in this?"

"What happens between the two of you is on you both. I will not interfere or invest a stake in it. I will caution the both of you, that if a war between you gets out of hand, and the police get involved, that will be bad for all parties, including me. And if I have to get involved, both of you will be unhappy, is that clear?" Both men nodded. "You better make sure none of my property is damaged in whatever you guys decide to do."

"No need to worry. It won't take long. If this guy comes

looking for us, he'll be eliminated before the week is over."

Vincent snickered, though he was careful to keep it inside. Billings had no idea what he was getting himself into. He was secretly hoping that Recker would make good on his threat, though he had to give the public image of being neutral. At least for now. If at some point in the future it made sense for him to get involved, if Recker had eliminated over half of them for instance, then Vincent might throw his weight behind the Silencer. But not yet.

"We done here?" Billings asked.

"I've said all I need to," Recker answered.

A little hot under the collar, Billings got up and stormed angrily out of the room. He wasn't used to being threatened and didn't take very kindly to it. After he'd left, Recker looked to his two hosts.

"That went well," Recker said.

The three remaining men got up and walked toward each other. Vincent was still a bit puzzled as to the merits of the meeting. It didn't seem to him like it accomplished anything.

"Can I ask why you asked for this meeting?" Vincent asked.

"Just wanted to meet the guy in person," Recker said. "Let him know I was coming."

"Seems like a peculiar move for you."

"How so?"

"A group such as this, I find it odd you would want them to know you're coming and be actively looking for you. I've known you a long time now. It seems to go against everything you usually do. You're a man who likes to operate in the shadows. This was anything but that."

"Sometimes you have to change tactics. Be a little unpredictable."

"What do you think this meeting actually accomplished?"

"Not much."

Vincent knew there was more to the story, but he wasn't going to press him on it. He knew he wouldn't get an answer anyway, even if he did. And if he got an answer, it probably wouldn't be the right one.

"Well, I'll be seeing you guys," Recker said.

Vincent and Malloy stayed put as they watched Recker leave the room.

"What do you think that was about?" Malloy asked. "Didn't make much sense. He had to know The Scorpions weren't gonna leave just because he wanted them to."

"No, this had a deeper meaning behind it."

"But what?"

"This benefitted him somehow," Vincent said. "He's obviously planning on taking them on full steam. This somehow gave him an edge. There's no other reason for it."

"I'm not seeing it."

"When it comes to our friend, there's quite a bit that we don't see."

"I dunno, I think maybe he's getting in over his head this time," Malloy said. "I mean, he's obviously as good as there is, but if he's planning on going up against eighty guys by himself, I have a feeling this may not end well for him."

"He's got help."

"Even so, the odds are still against them."

"I don't think he concerns himself much with the odds," Vincent said, continuing to think of what Recker was planning. "That's what this was about. Somehow, this lowered those odds."

Malloy scratched his head. "I dunno. I hope he knows what he's doing."

"If there's one thing we know about him... he doesn't do anything haphazardly. There's always a reason."

"Well, if The Scorpions assume it's just him, that'll let Haley sneak up on them. It's still just one man though."

Vincent squinted, his mind becoming clearer as his thoughts focused in on what Recker's plans were. "One man."

"What's that?"

"Perhaps this meeting was just a diversion for something else."

"What kind of diversion?"

"Well if we both agree this meeting was basically meaningless, and there was obviously another reason behind it, put yourself in his shoes. If you were him, why would you do this? Don't forget you are not alone in this pursuit."

Malloy thought for a moment. "I would try to get ahead of these guys. Start hitting them where they don't expect it. Lower the odds."

"And how would you do that if you didn't know where they were?"

"Put the word out. I'd figure someone out there's gotta know something about where they are."

"And if you didn't want to wait for what possibly may not come?" Vincent asked. "What if you wanted to be more proactive?"

"I'd probably find a way to..." Malloy looked at his boss, thinking he finally put his finger on it. "If I had a partner, I might figure out a way to tail them so I can find out where their base of operations is."

Vincent nodded, pleased that his underling was thinking along the same lines as him. "I agree."

"You think that's what's going on? You think Haley's out there too?"

"If I was a betting man, I'd probably be putting down some money on that."

"So, what do you wanna do?"

"Nothing. Let it play out."

"What if they start hitting The Scorpions and they think we're involved? It'll drag us into it right away, long before we're ready to engage."

"That's why I was clear to mention that we were staying neutral in their altercation."

"But are we?"

"For the moment," Vincent replied. "But like I told Recker before, if there's something we can do quietly to help, we'll give it to him."

"Why not just stay out of it completely and let him handle it on his own?"

"The whole devil you know versus the devil you don't know thing. Although I suppose in this case that we know both devils. It's just that one of them is one that we know we can work with and the other one is one that we know will eventually kill us if they get the chance."

"We don't even know where The Scorpions are setting up shop yet. Recker's gonna beat us to it."

"Seems very likely at this point. We'll continue to remain in the background, waiting for an opportune time. In support of that, have our friends in the police department get ready. We'll keep them abreast of what we know."

"Will do."

"I may not be ready to personally lift a finger against The Scorpions right now, but I'll be damned if I'm just gonna let them waltz into my city and take over."

9

Recker drove back to the office, though he kept in communication with Haley as he did. Haley let him know that he wasn't able to plant the tracking device and was following Billings instead. It'd been about twenty minutes and Haley reported that they still hadn't come to a stop yet.

"Where's this guy going?" Recker asked.

"I dunno. Doesn't seem like he does either," Haley said.

"You think he's made you?"

"No, I don't think so."

"He's probably just being extra careful."

"Could be. Either that or they're setting up base a good distance away."

"Yeah, could be. I'm just about at the office. Let me know if anything changes."

"Will do."

Recker arrived at the office five minutes later. Jones was standing near the door to let him in, waiting for him to get back.

"I just talked to Chris," Recker said. "He's still tailing Billings."

"Yes, I know. I just talked to him as well."

Recker could see something was bothering Jones by the worried expression on his face. "What's the matter?"

"Oh, it's nothing really."

"Don't give me that. I know when something's on your mind too you know."

Jones went over to the desk and sat down. "I guess I'm just worried."

"About what?"

"Just about Chris. I'm just hoping that he's not being led into a trap or something along those lines."

"A trap?"

"Yes," Jones said. "What if Billings knows he's being followed and is leading whoever it is into an ambush?"

Recker really didn't think about that possibility. Or he didn't put much thought into it if it ever entered his mind for even a second. "Chris is too good to let that happen. He knows how to trail someone without giving himself up. I'd bet my life on it."

"Hopefully, he doesn't have to."

Recker figured Jones was being a bit melodramatic. He always was a bit of a worrywart. Still, Recker guessed he had reason to. It was good for one of them to worry more than the others, he thought. Three people who were always gung-ho and charged right ahead on everything probably wouldn't work out too well. Jones' patience was the perfect balance for the team. They anxiously waited for Haley to check back in. They didn't want to keep talking to him and risk him losing his concentration and take the chance of getting spotted, so they just sat there and tried to keep busy until he called back. It turned out to be a long wait. It was another thirty minutes until Haley called back. Recker answered quickly.

"Hey, you all right?"

"Yeah, I'm good," Haley answered.

"Where you at?"

"Cheltenham."

"Cheltenham? What the hell are you doing there?"

"I dunno. This is where Billings went."

"So, he did go out of the city. Where's he at?"

"I assume it's his apartment or something. Either that or it's a friend, girlfriend, another member of the group, something like that. Whatever the case, he's at an apartment complex."

"Considering he just came from a meeting, I kind of doubt it's a friend or girlfriend," Recker said. "It's gotta either be his own place or some type of business."

"Yeah, he just went inside about two minutes ago. I'm kind of hanging back a little. I don't wanna get too close and blow it."

"You still got that tracking device, right?"

"Yeah."

"Why don't you just walk by his car and plant it? Can you do that?"

Haley waited a second before answering, looking at his surroundings. "Uh, maybe. I'm not exactly sure what apartment he went in, so I don't know if he's looking at it or not."

"Might have to take a chance."

"I'll give it a few minutes, just in case he's watching to see if he was tailed. If he's not out in ten minutes, I'll probably give it a shot."

"All right, let us know."

Recker turned to Jones to let him know, but he was already ahead of him. Jones was listening and started working as soon as he heard Recker repeat the area.

"I know, he's in Cheltenham," Jones said.

"A little outside of the city."

"But not too far. It would make sense not wanting to be directly in the city, so they don't inadvertently step on Vincent's toes, but still close enough to do some damage when they want to and be right on the doorstep for when they decide they want to take more territory."

"Really didn't anticipate him going to an apartment after the meeting," Recker said.

"Why not?"

Recker shrugged. "I don't know. I just assumed he'd go to his buddies and let them know what happened."

"Perhaps the other leaders of the group live there."

"Guess anything's possible."

"So, what was your opinion of Mr. Billings?" Jones asked.

"My opinion of Billings is that I think he's a grade A punk. Classic case of a guy who thinks he's tough and can do whatever he wants to anybody."

"I believe that is par for the course for that group. Probably don't let anyone in who doesn't think that way."

"Could be."

"If Chris is able to plant the tracker on Billings' car, exactly what is your plan after that?"

"I only got one plan," Recker answered.

"Which is?"

"To take as many of them out as quickly as possible."

"Even if we're successful a few times, it's quite possible that they might find the tracker."

"Anything's possible."

"Do you plan on taking out Billings first?"

"I'm an equal opportunity trash taker-outer. Don't really care who's first or who's last. As long as the job gets done."

Using the tracking device that Haley already had on, and was still in his car, Jones was able to bring up the address for the apartment complex in Cheltenham. He started digging through records to see if he could pin down any new tenants in the last couple of weeks. As he was doing that, Haley continued sitting in his car for about ten minutes, just as he said he would. There were probably about twenty cars between his and Billings.

Figuring enough time had elapsed since Billings had went inside, Haley grabbed the tracking device and got out of the car. He slowly walked toward the target car, not wanting to move too quickly in case someone was watching, making it obvious that he was up to something. Haley walked past several cars, and the front of the apartment building, before finally coming to Billings' car. Haley just stood there for a few moments and turned his head in every direction. He didn't notice any eyes looking back at him. He then meandered to the rear of the car, then slipped down to conceal himself behind the trunk and bumper. The tracking device was about the size of a memory card, making it fairly easy to put on, with Haley choosing to adhere it to the back of the license plate so it wouldn't be visible. After making sure it was secure, he had to get out of there quickly. Haley had no sooner stood up when he saw Billings, along with two other men, exit the building.

"Ah, crap," Haley muttered.

"Hey!" Billings yelled. "What are you doing by my car?!"

Haley had only two options at that point. He could either run, or he could try to play it cool, pretending like he didn't know what he was talking about. Both options had their risks. At the distance they were, it was unlikely he was going to outrun them and get to his car in time. They'd also probably assume that Haley did something to the car, which would result in them checking it, possibly finding the tracking device, though they still might not have found it. If he stayed and played the innocent card, and they didn't believe him, he'd still be looking at bad odds with men who were assumed to be pretty dangerous. After briefly thinking of the repercussions of either move, Haley chose to stay put. With him standing still, Billings and his two associates moved towards him.

"This your car?" Haley asked, as the men were now only a few feet away from him.

"Yeah."

"It's nice. I just drove in and saw it, came over to check it out."

"Who are you?" Billings asked.

"Oh, my name's Dave. Live in the building. Second floor."

Billings looked back at the building, not sure he bought what the man was selling yet. "It's just a regular car, man, nothing special to it."

"Yeah, the color and style just struck me all of a sudden. No offense meant or anything."

"So, you live here?"

"Yeah."

"Let's see your license," Billings said.

"My what?"

"Your license. I wanna make sure you actually do live here."

"Wouldn't do you any good," Haley said. "Just moved in last week. Haven't got the address switched over yet."

"Convenient. Let's see it, anyway."

"Why?"

"Because I wanna make sure you are who you say you are."

"Who else would I be?"

"I dunno," Billings answered. "Could be a number of people. Let's see it."

"No, I don't think so."

"You take that attitude and I'm gonna assume you got some other purpose for being near my car."

"I wasn't trying to steal it man, jeez."

"That's not what I thought."

Haley put his hands up. "All right, man, forget it. Let's just go our separate ways."

Billings quickly took a gun out of his belt and pointed it at Haley. "Just hold on there, buddy."

"Hey, what's that for? You're taking things a little far here, don't you think?"

"What were you doing by my car?"

"Nothing. I was just looking at it."

Billings held his gun a little firmer, pointing it straight at Haley's chest. "You better start talking right now or you're not gonna have another chance in a minute."

Haley looked at the two men standing next to Billings, neither of whom had their gun out yet, though he assumed they both had one. He realized there was no talking himself out of this one. If he was going to get free of this situation, he was going to have to shoot his way out. He just had to get to his gun first. Not an easy proposition when someone already had their gun pointed at him.

"All right, all right," Haley said. "You wanna see who I really am?" Billings didn't respond. He just stared at Haley with a distrustful look in his eye. "I'll reach into my back pocket and take out my wallet so you can look at my license, OK?"

Billings nodded. "Just do it slowly."

"All right, just don't get an itchy trigger finger or anything."

"You a cop or something?"

"No."

Haley slowly reached his arm around his back, putting his hand inside his back pocket to remove his wallet. He took his wallet out and gently brought it back around to the front of him and held it out. Billings grabbed hold of it, taking his eyes off his target for a second. As Billings brought it closer to him, Haley reached his arm around his back again, this time getting his fingers on the handle of his gun. Just as Billings had opened his wallet, Haley swiftly withdrew his gun and brought it to the front of him. Billings had lazily let his gun drop a few inches when he took the wallet, leaving him in a bad spot as the fight started. He dropped the wallet as he brought his gun back up, though Haley fired first, drilling a hole in Billings' chest, dropping him to the ground instantly. As the gun flew out of his hands, Haley's sights then turned to the two assistants. They each started reaching for their guns, but Haley was too quick for them considering his gun was already out. Haley took out the man to his left, then immediately did the same to the man on the right, neither giving him much opposition.

Haley stood there for a second, looking at the three men, disappointed with himself for letting it get to that situation. "Damn."

He wasn't sure the tracking device would be of much use now, but decided to let it stay, just in case the car passed down to another member of the group. Knowing he had to go soon with the police likely on the way, Haley reached down and grabbed his wallet, then jogged back to his car. Once back in his car, he quickly turned the engine on and got out of the parking lot, driving only across the street to a different apartment complex, and taking up one of the parking spots so he could keep an eye on what was happening with the chaos that he just left. As he sat there waiting, he called the office to let them know what was going on. Jones put the call on speaker.

"Chris, has the tracker been planted?" Jones asked.

"Uh, yeah, yeah, it's on. But there's been a complication."

"Oh. What's wrong?"

"Billings and two other guys came out just as I was putting the device on."

"Oh no. You said you put it on though?"

"Yeah. After I did, they came out, saw me near the car, came up to me and started asking questions."

"Since we're having this conversation, I assume you were able to talk your way out of it," Recker said.

"Not quite. Billings pulled a gun on me, wanted to know what I was doing there, started asking stuff. He knew something was up."

Recker and Jones looked at each other, knowing their plan failed. "So, what happened?" Jones asked.

"Since he had a gun on me, I had to come up shooting."

Jones' shoulders slumped, already knowing there were most likely fatalities involved. "And?"

"All three men went down."

Jones sighed, frustrated that their plan seemingly failed, though he was glad Haley made it out OK. "Are you hurt or anything?"

"No, I'm good. Just... ticked off I couldn't get the job done."

"You got the job done," Recker said. "They just happened to come out at the wrong time. It happens. We knew something like that was a possibility. Nothing you could do about it."

"Yeah, I guess. I just feel like maybe I could've played it differently."

"You did what had to be done," Jones said.

Jones knew that Haley was not a man who liked to shoot first and ask questions later. Unlike Recker, it was usually not Haley's first strategy. If Haley was involved in a shooting, Jones knew it had to be done and there was likely no other way out.

"I kept the tracker on the car though," Haley said. "Figured even if Billings is dead, maybe the car will pass down to one of the other members."

"That's good thinking," Recker said. "Could happen."

"Guess it's the only shot we got now, huh?"

"Where you at right now?"

"Across the street," Haley replied. "Just waiting to see what shakes down from this."

"The most important thing is that you're OK, and they're not," Jones said. "We'll figure out the next plan of attack from here."

"They all dead?" Recker asked.

"I'm not sure," Haley answered. "I didn't really get

enough time to check. I split pretty quickly. Didn't want to be seen."

"We'll monitor it," Jones said.

"I'll say this, though, if they're not, they're pretty lucky. I hit each of them at close range."

"Why don't you get back here, and we can figure out where we're going next."

"I'll wait a few more minutes and see what's going on here. See if these guys go to the hospital or the morgue."

"OK. As soon as that happens, get back here."

"Will do."

After they hung up, Recker and Jones just looked at each other for a moment, neither saying a word. Finally, after a minute, Jones broke the silence.

"So that's that."

"Sure is," Recker said.

"If they're not dead, we're going to have a new problem."

"What's that?"

"They can identify him."

"I doubt they'll be doing much talking to the police."

"Even if they don't, they'll know his face now," Jones said.

"I think we got bigger problems than that."

"Which would be?"

"This was our one chance to act in the shadows with them. If that car doesn't stay in Scorpions hands, we'll never get another shot at it. They'll know it was me, or that Haley was working in conjunction with me. We'll never get another meeting to try something like this again. Next time they'll shoot first."

"I guess our next step is just waiting to see if these three are alive or dead. If they are still alive, we might still be in business."

"Yeah."

"If not, we will have to alter our course."

"If not, then we'll just have to make sure their buddies join them."

10

Haley was back at the office, the group trying to keep tabs on the Scorpions who had been shot. He saw two of them taken away in an ambulance, which meant they were still alive, even if it was only briefly. One of them was taken away in a body bag. Jones was the one who was doing most of the checking, as Recker and Haley kept their time focused on trying to locate the rest of the group. They were digging into the apartment records that Billings was found at, that Jones had previously pulled up, going through them to see if there were any other members living there that could be identified.

"How's things looking on our friends?" Recker casually asked, not really that concerned about them. For some reason, the silence in the room was getting to him. Usually he craved the silence. Now, he wished for anything but. Maybe because he felt like it was making him think too much about alternatives.

"Nothing definite yet," Jones answered. "They were taken to Washington Hospital. As far as I can see they are still listed as critical."

"Where?" Recker asked, a touch of concern plainly evident on his face.

"Washington." Jones wasn't sure what the problem was. "Is there something wrong with that?"

Recker didn't answer at first. It was obvious something heavy was on his mind though.

"Michael?" Jones asked, starting to get worried himself that something was wrong.

"Mia's there."

"What do you mean, Mia's there? She doesn't work at that hospital."

"They were short-handed this week. They put a call out to other hospitals in the area to see if anyone was interested in helping out a few days."

"So, she went?"

"Yeah. You know her. Always wants to help people."

"Well, I'm sure everything will be fine. It's not like she will be having any interaction with him or anything."

"I hope not."

"Besides, from what I can gather, the police are already guarding him," Jones said.

"What?"

"If Billings survives, he's being charged with a felony."

"How's that work?"

"Apparently when he was found he still had a gun in his hand. He's a convicted felon. That's illegal."

"Wow, they're really stretching it on that one," Recker

said. "They find a guy there almost dead and they charge him with a crime."

"Is it a technicality? Perhaps. It's also using all the tools at your disposal to get a dangerous criminal off the streets. Do you disagree with that?"

"No. You do what you gotta do, no matter what it takes."

They both went back to working their respective computers, though Jones periodically looked over at his friend, still seeing a worried look on his face.

"Mia will be fine," Jones said.

"Yeah."

"It's not the first time she's been at a hospital when a dangerous criminal is brought in."

"I know," Recker said.

They dropped the subject and went back to work again, though Recker was interrupted from his after about twenty minutes, with his phone ringing. He looked surprised at seeing Vincent's name, as he usually didn't call directly unless there was an emergency. If it wasn't urgent, he usually had Malloy call for him to set something up first. Recker got up as he answered the call, beginning to walk around the room.

"To what do I owe the honor of this call?" Recker said.

"I just wanted to clarify a few things."

"Like what?"

"The biggest thing is I heard about what happened to Billings. Was that your doing?"

"If you're asking whether I pulled the trigger, then no, I did not."

"Strange that it happened within hours after your meeting," Vincent said.

"It is what it is."

"Perhaps it was your partner."

"Perhaps."

"You know, it occurred to me after you left, that maybe you set up the meeting so you could follow him."

"Good thinking," Recker said.

"Is that what happened?"

Recker cleared his throat, wondering if he should admit it or not. "Listen, whatever happened with Billings, I'm sure whoever it was, it wasn't their intent to get into a shootout with him. In fact, I would bet that Billings forced their hand and didn't leave them any other choice. With that being said, the man got what he deserved."

"I can appreciate that. I just want to make sure that nothing will come back to me."

"Don't see how it would, considering the man met with me and I didn't do it."

"He'll be able to identify who shot him at some point though," Vincent said.

"I guess so, assuming he lives."

"He will."

"What makes you so sure?"

"I already got the word. He just came out of surgery a few minutes ago. He's gonna pull through."

"Doesn't matter," Recker said. "I hear the police are gonna charge him, so he's irrelevant now."

"I don't know about that."

"Why?"

"The police have a few men there guarding him, ready to take him in once he's well enough to move."

"Let me guess, a few of them are yours."

Vincent laughed. "Like I always say, it pays to have friends everywhere."

"Anyway, I doubt he's gonna do much cooperating with the police. Might tell his buddies, but he's not gonna swing any deals or anything."

"I agree. But I'm hearing Mr. Billings is a little more influential and important to the group than we've previously been led to believe."

"How so?"

"I've heard rumblings that The Scorpions will somehow try to get him out of police custody at some point."

"How they gonna manage that?" Recker asked.

"I don't know. I don't have any details. Like I said, it's just what I've heard."

"How'd you hear that already?"

"Like I said, Mike, friends in the right places. It pays. Just thought you would like to know, since if that's the case, I'm sure it would involve several members of the group. And if there was a person out there interested in eliminating a bunch of them at a time, they might like to know."

"Thanks. I'll pass the information along in case there is such a person."

"Good. Be safe, Mike."

"Always."

After getting off the phone, Recker went over to the

window and stared out, thinking about everything he'd just been told. Jones let him alone for a few minutes before finally trying to get it out of him.

"May I ask what that was in reference to?"

Recker turned around and looked at his partners. "Vincent says Billings is already out of surgery. He pulled through."

"Lucky for him," Haley said.

"Lucky indeed," Jones said. "Well, instead of death he's looking at a prison sentence instead."

"Maybe," Recker replied.

"What do you mean?"

"Vincent says he's heard rumblings that The Scorpions are gonna try and get him out of police custody somehow."

"That sounds like a tall order to me."

"He says they're gonna try it."

"Like I said, it sounds like a tall order."

"We'll see. Doesn't mean they won't try it though."

"I'm sure if Vincent's heard about it then the police have as well," Haley said.

"Could be."

"I'm sure they'll have adequate protection for him," Jones said.

"What would you consider adequate?"

"I don't know. It doesn't really matter as far as we're concerned though, does it?"

"It will if he somehow manages to escape," Recker answered.

"I think we're getting a little far ahead of ourselves.

Him escaping still seems far fetched to me."

"Guess we'll see."

"What about Tyrell?" Haley asked. "Maybe he's picked up something."

"That's a good idea. I'll give him a call." Recker picked up his phone again and called Tyrell.

"Hey, whatcha want this time?" Tyrell asked. "Want me to throw myself in a snake pit or something?"

Recker laughed. "Why do you always assume the worst whenever I call?"

"Because I know you."

"Fair enough."

"So whatcha got?"

"One of the Scorpions was shot and taken to Washington Hospital earlier."

"Yeah, I already heard something about that," Tyrell said. "Was that you guys?"

"You know a good shooter doesn't kiss and tell."

"Yeah, right."

"Anyway, I just talked to Vincent, and he said he's heard rumbling that The Scorpions are gonna try and free this guy from custody."

"That's bold."

"You hear anything about it?"

"Nah. Don't mean it won't happen though. Vincent's probably the only guy in this city plugged in better than I am."

"Yeah, I was just hoping you might have heard more details," Recker said.

"No, haven't heard nothin'. I'll keep checking around

though, see if I can come up with something. Just have to be careful with these guys, 'cause if they hear someone's poking around in their business, there's usually a price to be paid right after that. And that's one bill I really don't wanna receive right now."

"I hear ya. Just keep your ears open."

"Definitely will, my man."

Recker hung up, and Haley could see on his face that he didn't get a positive answer. But he figured he would ask, anyway.

"Hasn't heard anything?"

"No," Recker replied. "He'll keep digging."

"Well, guess there's nothing else to do right now but wait until something breaks."

"Yeah. That's all we can do right now. Just wait."

11

M ia was on her break, sitting alone at a table in the cafeteria. She'd been texting Recker off and on, who alerted her to the situation with Billings.

"Everything's fine, Mike. I'm sure if something happens, they'll wait until he's out of here."

"I know. I just want to make sure you're OK."

"I'm fine. I'm just on my break."

"Haven't seen anything weird?"

"I work at a hospital all day. I see weird stuff all the time."

"Lol. I know. I meant weird... even for you."

"No, everything's fine. Relax."

"I'll try. How's everything else there?"

"Not much different than usual. I mean, it's dealing with the same stuff, just talking to different people. Everyone's been nice though."

"Good."

"I'm gonna finish eating, then get back to work."

"OK. When are you done?"

"In about four hours."

"OK. I'll try to meet you at home by the time you get there."

"Sounds good. I'll see you later. Love you."

"Love you too."

Recker put his phone down and continued staring at it, causing Jones to look at him out of the corner of his eye.

"Everything OK?" Jones asked.

"Yeah."

"Stop worrying."

"I'm not worried."

Jones stopped typing and fully turned his head toward him. "Oh, really?"

"Not... that much."

"It's been a couple hours," Haley said. "And we haven't heard any other chatter. Could be they gave up on the plan. Couldn't find a way to make it work."

"One thing about The Scorpions is once their mind's made up, they'll find a way to make it work. I gotta believe that if the rumors are out there, in this case it's true. They're bold enough to try it, whether it has a good chance of working or not."

"Well if something happens, I'm sure we'll hear about it," Jones said.

"I just hope we don't hear it after it's too late."

Mia had just put her tray away and started walking toward the door when the lights started flickering. She stopped and looked up at the ceiling. It made her a little nervous considering what Recker was talking to her about. But considering the lights were still on, she chalked it up to just one of those things. She had just walked through the swinging doors and stood in the hallway when she heard a woman screaming. She looked down the hallway, then saw the woman come into view.

"There's men with guns!" the woman yelled.

Mia stood there motionless as the woman ran past her. Though the hallway was usually a pretty packed place, it was eerily quiet now. Wanting to get back to her floor, she ran over to the elevator and pressed the button. Once she got to the fourth floor of the ten-story building, the elevator suddenly stopped, and the doors opened. There was nobody getting on though. Mia stepped out and looked around, not seeing anything unusual. There were doctors, nurses, patients, all walking by. Nobody seemed to be aware of anything unusual going on. Mia went over to the station desk where one of the nurses was standing.

"Have you guys heard anything about someone with a gun in the building?"

"What?" the nurse replied. "No, I haven't heard anything like that."

"Oh, OK. Must've been a false alarm or something."

Mia turned around to get back on the elevator, but the lights went off, and the elevator door closed. A few seconds later, one of the buzzers started sounding, a loud screeching noise that went off every two seconds, with an accompanying red light that started blinking in every hallway. An announcement then came over the intercom.

"This is hospital security. We have an emergency situation. There are armed men in the building. Please stay inside your rooms and lock them. Do not attempt to leave the hospital and do not attempt to roam the hallways for your own safety. We will let you know when it is safe to exit again. Again, stay in your present location and lock your doors."

Doctors, nurses, patients, and visitors all started scrambling around, trying to take whatever kind of cover they could. The hospital staff first tried to get everyone in the hallway or in a waiting area into a room. Once most everyone was secure, a few of the doctors and nurses, including Mia, huddled together to come up with a plan.

"OK, first we have to figure out which patients need something immediately," a doctor said. "Just in case we're barricaded for an hour or two and not able to leave our rooms, and a patient desperately needs something, we're able to give them what they need. So, let's quickly figure out who needs what and grab it now."

They went over to the station and started looking at charts, hoping to get the medicine they needed quickly, not knowing exactly where the danger was lurking. It turned out that it was lurking everywhere. Around forty Scorpions had entered the building, locking and blocking entrances and exits, taking out the security room with the cameras to hide their movements. Two men remained at each entrance to make sure nobody came in or out. The rest started going up and down each floor. It wasn't known which floor Billings was on, as it was being kept a secret, but they also knew there were police officers in the building guarding him.

Less than three minutes later, gunfire erupted on the fifth floor, as The Scorpions found their target. There were four police officers on the floor, and they were quickly overwhelmed by the amount of men they were facing. The Scorpions were heavily armed and meant business. The battle between the two sides lasted several minutes as bullets flew everywhere, hospital staff and patients taking cover under beds, in bathrooms, wherever they could find, as bullets penetrated through some of the doors.

On the fourth floor, as the staff was looking through charts, one of the doors that led to a staircase opened up, several Scorpions stepping out. As soon as they were in sight, most of the staff scattered, finding the nearest door that they could get behind. Only three nurses stayed in their spot, Mia included. As two of The Scorpions cleared the floor, the other one came up to the desk and looked at the nurses. The man was tall, well-built, bald, sunglasses on, and chewing gum. If there ever was a tough-looking guy, he was it. As the man looked at him, he listened to the radio that was clipped to his belt.

"Hey, who's nearby that has a doctor or nurse in sight?" a man asked.

The man picked up his radio. "I got three nurses standing in front of me."

"Bring them to the fifth floor."

"Ten-four."

"All right, you three are coming with me."

The youngest of the three nurses, just barely on the

job for a month, instantly looked terrified. She started shaking her head and backing up.

"No," she said. "I can't."

"You can and you will," the man said.

"No, please."

The man, armed with an assault rifle, brought the weapon up in front of him and pointed it at the young lady. He looked like he didn't mind using it if he had to.

"Last chance," he said.

Mia jumped in front of her, with her arms up. "She'll come. She'll come. Just relax." The man lowered his weapon slightly as Mia turned around to look at her young counterpart. She put her hands on the nurse's arms to calm her down. "Listen, everything will be fine if we just do what they ask, OK?"

"I don't know."

"We don't have a choice right now. Just calm down, do what they say, and everyone will get out of this alive. But you gotta calm down."

The young nurse nodded. "OK."

Mia turned around to the bald-headed Scorpion. "We're coming."

The man had a smug look on his face and pointed with his head. "Up the stairs. Just so we're clear, you do anything other than exactly what I tell you, or you try something stupid, you'll leave this hospital in a body bag."

"Understood," Mia replied. "Everyone's fine."

"Let's go."

The nurses complied with his directions and started moving to the stairwell, the big man walking behind them to make sure they did as he wanted. Once they got to the fifth floor, they immediately saw what could have been close to a hundred people sitting on the floor. Doctors, nurses, patients, visitors, anyone who wasn't tied to a bed or needed to be on one for medical purposes, they were all rounded up. There were ten Scorpions wandering around on the floor.

"What's this about?" Mia asked.

The bald man behind her just pushed her further into the room by shoving his rifle into her back. "Just move and sit down."

The nurses sat down with the rest of the bunch, who were lined up throughout the hallway. The tough-looking man that brought them up then sought out one of his friends.

"What's going on, why are we waiting? What's taking so long?"

An equally tough-looking man responded. "One of the doctors said Tommy shouldn't be moved yet. They said he needs to rest for at least two or three more hours to give his body a little more time to recuperate."

The bald man chewed on his gum. "I don't know if we got that kind of time. Cops'll be swarming on this place in a few minutes most likely."

"That's fine. Whether we leave now or in a couple hours won't affect our getaway plans at all."

"Except what happens if they swarm the building before then?"

"Then we'll deal with it. I didn't come in here to get him just to watch him die getting him out. We'll wait a couple hours. If we need to buy some time, we'll buy some time."

Mia, looking around at the other workers, immediately thought of the patients. She put her hand up, just like she was back in school, to ask a question. The two men talking noticed her move and looked at her.

"What do you want?" the bald man asked.

"I heard you talking about being here for a few hours."

"So?"

"What about the patients who need care?" Mia asked. "What about them? We have to be able to take care of them. We can't just leave them."

The second man took his pistol out of his belt and pointed it at her and fired. Mia was instantly knocked over by the force of the bullet and held her stomach as she lay on her back. The bald-headed man continued chewing his gum, though he looked at his partner with a little disgust, thinking it wasn't really necessary.

"Anybody else got any questions?" the second man asked. There wasn't a sound to be heard. "Drag her out of here."

One of the other Scorpions came over to Mia's body and grabbed her by the back of the shirt and drug her across the floor, blood smearing all over it, pulling her into a nearby patient room that was empty. The rest of the staff members looked on in horror, stunned by what they'd just seen. A few people started crying.

"If anyone else has any questions, remember this moment," the second man said. "Remember it good."

12

Though the room Mia was brought into had no patients inside, there was a doctor and a nurse seated on the floor by the door. As soon as the man bringing her in left, the doctor immediately started working on her.

"She's already lost a good amount of blood," the nurse said.

The doctor sighed, not liking the situation. "If this thing doesn't end soon and we don't get her on an operating table, I'm not sure she's going to last too long."

Only a minute after the doctor started working on Mia, the bald-headed man that brought her up from the fourth floor appeared in the frame of the door. The doctor and nurse each stopped working on Mia, fearful of what might happen, thinking they might be the next victims, and they put their arms halfway up. The man, holding his rifle out in front of him, just looked at them and nodded.

He then disappeared back into the hallway, allowing the doctor to get back to work on Mia.

"First thing we gotta do is stop the bleeding," the doctor said. "Look around for bandages, tape, anything we can use."

Though weak and losing more energy by the second, Mia somehow managed to put her hand in her pocket and remove her phone. Her hand was shaking, but she held the phone in the air to get the doctor's attention.

"Just relax," the doctor told her.

"Take... take my phone," Mia wearily said. The doctor begrudgingly took it, though he really just wanted her to calm down. "Call Mike... he will come."

"Who's Mike?"

"Let him know... what happened... he will come."

"Oh no," Jones said, suddenly shifting positions in his seat as if something had just grabbed his attention. He was getting the attention of his two partners by his mannerisms though.

"What?" Recker asked.

Jones only briefly looked at him, though he didn't answer, and continued looking at his computer. Haley got up from his chair and walked over to him, standing behind him.

"What is it?" Haley asked.

Jones licked his lips and cleared his throat before

responding. He knew what he was about to say would not go over well.

"It seems that Washington Hospital has been overtaken and is under siege."

"What do you mean it's under siege?" Recker asked. "From who?"

"Reports are coming out that the hospital is currently under control of a group of armed men who stormed the building not too long ago."

"It's The Scorpions. It's gotta be. This is what they had in mind to get Billings out."

Jones put his hand on his head and started rubbing his forehead. Everyone's mind immediately turned to Mia, praying for her safety, though it was in nobody's mind more than Recker's.

"Any casualties?" Recker asked.

"There's been no reports yet that I can find," Jones said.

Jones grabbed a remote for the TV and put it on, assuming there would be some coverage about it on the screen. They were right. They turned it on just in time to hear a reporter talking about how the police had locked down the perimeter and had the building surrounded.

"I'm sure she's OK," Jones said, knowing it was on his friend's mind. "Mia's a resourceful person. She'll find a way through it."

"That's not what bothers me," Recker replied.

"What does?"

"She naturally tries to stand up for what's right. What happens if someone near her gets out of line and angers one of the Scorpions and she tries to protect them? And she would."

"Yes, I know. Let's just pray that everyone keeps their head and they get what they want and leave without any fatalities."

"That means losing Billings," Haley said.

"So be it," Jones said. "We can get him another time. We still have the tracking device planted. We can latch on to him again. We can't replace any lives being lost in that building."

"Looks like it's a standoff that's gonna last a while."

"Quite a while. The police aren't likely to rush into that building without knowing exactly what they're up against."

"Plus, there's hostages involved," Recker said. "They're not gonna risk losing all those people by storming the building. A lot of innocent people would wind up getting killed."

"This might go on for a day or two."

"Nobody can let it go on for that long. Bigger question is what they want with that building."

"What do you mean?" Haley asked.

"If all they wanted was Billings, why take the building hostage? Why not just grab your target and go?"

"Maybe Billings isn't well enough to be moved yet," Jones answered. "The man just had major surgery. Perhaps they are giving him a little more time to recover before moving him."

"Could be."

Before they could discuss it any further, Recker's

phone beeped, indicating he had a text message. As soon as he saw it was Mia, he breathed a sigh of relief.

"It's Mia," Recker said.

The others could almost hear the weight being lifted off his shoulders as he said her name. The hopefulness that they had faded away quickly as they continued looking at Recker's face, which was now looking as concerned as ever.

"What is it?" Haley asked.

Recker didn't answer, instead reading the message again.

"I don't know why, but Mia asked me to contact you to let you know what's going on here. Mia has been shot and is badly wounded and needs urgent care that we cannot give while these armed men have control of the hospital. She said to contact you because you would come. I don't know who you are, but please help us."

Recker's heart felt like it had just dropped out of his chest. He started breathing heavily and stumbled backwards onto his seat. His eyes darted all around the room, at least as far as they could go without him turning his head. There were so many thoughts and emotions swirling around inside him at the moment that it felt like his head was going to explode. He couldn't lose her. He finally got a moment of clarity and his mind went back to the dream he had of Mia dying in the hospital right in front of him. Deeply concerned about what might have been happening, Haley walked over to Recker's chair and put his hand on his shoulder.

"What's wrong?"

Recker didn't respond. He just kept staring straight ahead.

"Mike, what's wrong?"

Recker finally looked up at his partner, though he had a kind of glossy look in his eye, like he wasn't really there. He was going to try to answer Haley's question, but he couldn't get any words out. Instead, Recker handed him his phone. Haley took it and read the message. Seeing the words on the screen was almost like a knife to his gut as well. He loved Mia like a sister. She had always been nice to him and did things for him, like decorating his apartment, cooking meals for him occasionally, just being there to talk to sometimes since there was nobody else to confide in. He had trouble comprehending the news as well.

Haley looked at Jones and tossed the phone to him so he could see what was going on as well, without anyone actually having to talk about it. As soon as Jones read it, a somber look overtook his face. He sat there thinking about what they could do. Jones looked at Recker, worried about what was to come. He knew Recker better than anybody. Though the man looked despondent at the moment, Jones knew that was going to change soon. At some point, something was going to kick in and Recker would switch gears. He would become something else. Something that couldn't be stopped. Jones was just waiting for that switch to flip.

Jones briefly turned his attention back to the computer to get the latest updates, then he heard it. He heard a fist pound itself into the desk, then turned and saw Recker unleash a few more shots upon it. Concerned about his well-being, Jones watched Recker go across the room until he got to his gun cabinet. Jones and Haley looked at each other, not knowing exactly what was going on, though they had a roundabout idea.

"What are you doing?" Jones asked.

He didn't get a reply.

"Mike, talk to us," Jones said. "We can't help you if you don't let us."

"I'm getting Mia."

"How do you plan to do that?"

"I don't know. I'll figure it out when I get there."

Jones was worried his friend wasn't thinking straight and was going to do something stupid and rush into the hospital and get himself killed. After a few minutes, Recker had a bag packed and was ready to go. He was ready for war, and he had the weapons to prove it. He started walking toward the door, not letting the others know anything else about what he was planning. Jones looked at Haley and nodded, wanting him to intercept Recker before he made it out the door. Haley rushed over to the door, getting there just before Recker had reached it. He put his hands on the front of Recker's shoulders to prevent him from getting past him.

"Get out of my way," Recker said.

"No, you can't do this," Haley replied.

"Chris, don't make me hurt you. Get out of my way."

"No, you can't just leave like this. You're not thinking straight and you're moving on pure emotion right now."

"That's right, I am. Mia's out there, bleeding, maybe

dying. I'm not sitting here waiting for that to happen. I'm going to get her. Get out of my way."

Recker tried to push Haley to the side, but he wouldn't budge. Haley just grabbed on tighter.

"I hear you, man, I hear you. We can both do this. But you gotta calm down so we can come up with a plan."

"I don't need a plan," Recker said. "Plans take time. Mia hasn't got it. I need to go now."

"Just give it ten minutes and we'll think of something so that we can get Mia, and we won't get killed in the process."

"Chris, I don't care about my own life right now. I need to save Mia. There might be too many guys there for us to take care of. You stay here and man the fort in case I don't make it back."

"No, that's not an option."

"I don't have time to argue about this."

"That's right, we don't have time to argue, so just listen to me. I love her too. We all love her. Nobody's saying to just leave her there. If you wanna roll in there and get her, then I'll roll in right beside you, brother. Let's just take a few minutes to figure out how to get her without it taking us all day to find her. *We* will get her. Let's just do it right. That's all I'm saying."

"And if we don't make it?" Recker asked. "What about everything here?"

Haley looked at Jones. "We'll make it."

Jones wasn't about to stand in their way, not when it came to Mia's life. "Chris is right. Mia's life takes precedence over everything. But let's find a way where all three of you make it back safely."

Recker took a deep breath and briefly looked at the both of them. "You're sure you wanna do this? We'll probably be badly outnumbered."

Haley took out the magazine from his pistol then jammed it back in. "Let's kick some ass."

13

Recker agreed to wait a few minutes to come up with some kind of plan, though he wouldn't wait any longer than that. The three huddled around the computer as Jones dug into the hospital building layout.

"Hospital cameras," Recker said. "If you can hack into the feed, we can see where everyone is at."

"That's a good idea," Jones said, instantly changing course.

Jones spent the next few minutes trying to get into the cameras at the hospital, though he wasn't having much luck. The faces he was making told the others all they needed to know about how he was progressing.

"No luck?" Recker asked.

Jones shook his head. "No, there's something wrong. I'm not able to get in."

"Cameras are down," Haley said. "Probably got taken

out already. Probably their first move when they got into the building."

"Probably," Recker replied, putting his hand on his head in frustration as he tried to think of something else.

"What else can we do?" Haley asked.

"It'd be a little easier if we knew where exactly Mia was," Jones said. "But since we don't..."

"Wait a minute. Why don't we?"

"What?"

"It's simple enough to find out, right? Just text back her number and ask."

Recker tapped Haley on the chest then pulled out his phone and quickly sent a message.

"I'm on my way. What floor are you on?"

The doctor answered almost immediately. *"5th. Who are you?"*

"How many are there?"

"Don't know. At least six or seven just on this floor. I think they're everywhere though."

"Just sit tight and take care of Mia. I will be there."

"What are you going to do?"

"Take them out."

"How?"

Recker didn't need to respond anymore. He'd gotten all the information that was relevant. "Fifth floor. At least six or seven Scorpions there."

"Multiply that by every floor and we could be looking at..."

"Too many. Doesn't matter though. I've gotta go."

"We just have to figure out how to get in. They've probably got people watching every entrance, and don't forget the police have the building surrounded, so you're going to have to avoid them too."

Recker stared at the screen. He wasn't sure how he was going to get in. He just knew he was. If he had to steal a tank and barrel right through the front entrance, that's what he would do. But with Mia in trouble, his mind wasn't thinking as clearly as it usually was.

"Not sure how much you'll wanna do this, but I got something," Haley said.

"What?" Recker replied.

"Vincent."

"What about him?"

"He's got men in the police department, right?"

"Yeah."

"And the police are outside that building, right?"

"Yeah."

"So maybe he's got men outside that building that can help get us in."

Recker nodded. "It's worth a shot. I'll try anything right now."

Recker grabbed his phone again and dialed Vincent's number. Luckily, the crime boss picked up right away.

"What can I do for you, Mr. Recker?"

"I need a favor and I need it right now."

Vincent could hear the urgency in Recker's voice and knew it was an emergency. "What is it?"

"Washington Hospital is under siege right now. The Scorpions have taken it over."

"Yes, I've heard. I guess this was their plan in getting Billings out of custody."

"Yeah, I don't even care about that right now," Recker said.

While normally he wouldn't want to divulge his reasons for doing anything, he was above playing games at the moment. He needed to express immediately why he needed to get into that building right away.

"So, what's this about?" Vincent asked.

"I need to get in there. Now."

"Why?"

"You know I have a girlfriend, Mia."

"I do."

"She's in that hospital right now," Recker said.

"Not to be doubtful or dubious of your reasons or anything, but I know for a fact she doesn't work in that hospital."

"She is this week. They had a staffing shortage, and she volunteered to work there this week."

"I'd say that's bad timing."

"Listen, I wouldn't be asking you this unless it was an emergency. I got a text from someone who said Mia's been shot. She's on the fifth floor of that building. Now if she's not able to text me herself, I know it's bad. I need to get in there."

"Ahh, the white knight coming to the rescue."

"I don't have time to talk," Recker said. "If you can't help me, that's fine. I just need to know now."

"How do you know she's really hurt?"

"What?"

"How do you know it's not a ploy just to get you in that building? Maybe they're aware of your relationship."

"No, it's not possible. No way. There's no way they would know."

"You're sure of that."

"Damn sure, yes."

"OK."

"Can you help me get into that building or not?"

"What makes you think I can help?"

"Really? The police have the building surrounded, you have police on your payroll, sometimes two plus two equals four."

"Indeed, it does."

"I don't have time for this. Can you help or not?"

"Give me five minutes," Vincent answered.

Recker sighed, not liking the answer. Everyone kept stalling him, asking him to wait a few more minutes. Each of these minutes added up.

"I don't have..."

"Just five minutes and I'll call you back," Vincent said.

"OK. But after that I'm gone."

"Understood."

Frustrated, Recker forcefully put his phone down on the table. The others could tell he didn't like whatever he heard in his conversation with Vincent.

"He can't help?" Haley asked.

"He said to give him five minutes."

"Well it's not a no."

"It's just additional time that we can't afford to waste."

"Maybe there's something he has to set up first?"

"Maybe. I just don't want to wait. Mia might not have five extra minutes."

"If he said to wait a few minutes, I'm sure he has a good reason," Jones said. "As much as I hate to say it, aligning with him on this matter might be the best possible solution."

Recker paced around the room for a few minutes, clutching his phone in his hand, as he waited for a call back. He tried to breathe normally and keep his emotions under check, but it was a hard thing to do, knowing that Mia was lying in a hospital somewhere bleeding. Five minutes came and went without a call, and Recker was as restless as ever. He was about to forego the call and just do what he wanted to do in the first place. The others could tell he wasn't waiting much longer and had to try to slow him down.

"Just give him a few more minutes," Haley said. "He'll call."

Recker sighed. "I keep telling you guys, Mia doesn't have five extra minutes here, three extra minutes there, ten extra minutes there. She needs help. And she needs it now."

"No one is disputing that, Michael," Jones replied.

"Then why are we just sitting here waiting? We need to be doing something. I can't just keep waiting here."

Recker was just about to make good on his words and head for the door when his phone suddenly started ringing again. He eagerly answered.

"Sorry for the delay," Vincent said. "It took a few minutes longer than I anticipated."

"What did?"

"I have a plan to get you in. That's as far as I can help you. After that it's up to you."

"That's fine. That's all that I need."

"Here's what we'll do. I've just sent Jimmy to the hospital. You'll meet him there in the parking lot adjacent to the hospital. It's just used for extra parking and is not in use at the moment."

"OK?"

"From there, you'll get in his car, and he'll drive into the underground parking garage at the hospital."

"Don't the police have it blocked off?" Recker asked.

"Jimmy will take care of that. Once you're there, there are two ways into the hospital. One is the elevator, but I believe that's out of order. The other is the stairs. It's likely it's either blocked off, or they have men stationed there, or maybe both. So, you might have to fight your way in."

"I expected that."

"But that also means you'll lose the element of surprise. They'll know you're there almost immediately."

"It's gotta be done."

"OK. I assume this is going to be a two-man job?"

"That's right," Recker answered.

"OK. I'll make sure you're outfitted properly."

"Thank you."

"You can thank me when you have her safely in your arms. For now, better get moving."

Recker put his phone away and went over to grab his bag. "We're up."

"What's the plan?" Jones asked.

"Malloy is going to meet us in a parking lot next to the hospital. From there, he'll drive us into the underground parking garage. So that'll get us through the police block."

"And the hospital? How are you getting in?"

"There's an entrance from the steps leading from the garage to the hospital. We'll have to use that."

"It's probably blocked, or they'll have men there."

"Most likely. But it's our only way. We'll have to take it. We're gonna have to fight our way in."

Recker looked over to Haley. "You ready?"

"Let's go. Let's go get her."

Jones watched his two friends fly out the door, hoping they'd return in the same manner in which they left. In one piece.

14

It took Recker and Haley about twenty-five minutes to get to the parking lot next to Washington Hospital. Once they arrived, there was a big empty lot without a single car in it. They picked a spot and parked to wait.

"You sure this is it?" Haley asked.

"That's what they said."

"Hopefully, he gets here soon."

A few seconds later their attention was drawn to a dark SUV pulling into the lot. It sped up until it reached Recker's car, then parked two spots next to him. Once Malloy got out of his vehicle, Recker and Haley did the same.

"How's it going boys?" Malloy asked.

"You know the situation?" Recker replied.

"Sure do. C'mon to the back."

Malloy went to the back of his truck and opened the trunk. He had several bags worth of stuff in there.

"You guys need guns?"

"We're good," Recker said. "You should know we're always packed."

Malloy laughed. "Yeah. Here, take these and put them on." Malloy handed them plain black, military style outfits, complete with armor and bullet-proof vests. He also gave them matching black ski masks with a hole cut out for their eyes.

"What's this for?" Haley asked.

"Gotta make a grand entrance. This has to be a rogue outfit in there doing this. I tried to get swat uniforms, but that was shot down. They need deniability for whatever goes on in there. So, the official story is nobody knows how you guys got in there or who you are. That's what the masks are for too. So, nobody can identify you. That's as much for The Scorpions as anyone else. If they don't know who hit them, they won't know who to target if any of them make it out."

"So how we getting in?" Recker asked.

"I know the cops who are guarding the entrance to the garage. They'll let me pass through. You guys will be in the back. Then it'll be go-time."

It all sounded good to Recker and Haley. They started getting dressed, then noticed Malloy doing the same.

"What are you doing?" Recker asked.

"What do you mean?" Malloy answered.

"Why are you changing too?"

"Because I'm going in with you."

"What?"

Malloy grinned. "You didn't think I'd let you go in and have all the fun yourself, did you?"

"You don't have to do this. It's not your fight."

"Hey, I don't want these guys in this city any more than you do. As far as I'm concerned, any opportunity we have to take these guys out, it's a shot worth taking."

"I don't know for sure how many are in there. There's no guarantee we're coming back out."

"I made my peace with that a long time ago," Malloy said. "You don't do what we do without expecting that to happen at some point. It's gonna happen, eventually. I'm good with it."

"You know why I'm going in?"

Malloy nodded. "Yeah. Let's get her and take a lot of them out in the process."

"Well, I'm not gonna try and stop you so, I guess you're in if that's what you want."

"That's what friends are for, right?"

"I suppose."

After the three men were finished putting on their black outfits, and their vests were on, they put on belts to hold their excess ammunition, figuring they were going to need a lot of it. They each strapped a pistol to a holster on each side of their leg, plus a backup weapon in the back of their belts. And they each had a rifle in hand. They looked like they were ready for a war. Recker reached into his bag and pulled out a suppressor and handed it to Malloy.

"What's this for?" Malloy asked.

"I wanna try and get in as quietly as possible," Recker replied. "If we go in bombs away, gunfire all over the place, they're gonna know we're there in two seconds. If we can try to go in quietly, we might have a better chance. At least we wouldn't have to fend off twenty guys at one time. Hopefully."

"Sounds good to me."

Recker looked at his two partners after he was done attaching his magazines to his belt. "Everyone ready?"

Haley nodded. "Ready to go," Malloy answered.

"OK, before we go in, I think we need to set a few things straight. If at any point I go down before we reach Mia, whether I'm badly injured, can't move, whatever, you guys leave me behind in order to get to her. Agreed?"

Haley and Malloy looked at each other, not thrilled with the idea, but both nodded and agreed, knowing that's what he really wanted. "I guess the same should go for us, huh?" Malloy said.

"Yeah," Haley said. "One other thing before we go."

"Yeah?" Recker said.

"What are we doing with any hostages we run into on the way? We can't just send them running into the hospital. They might run right into a bullet."

"And it's a cinch we can't take them with us," Malloy said.

Recker thought about it for a few seconds. "We tell them to sit tight until we have everything under control. We tell them to lock themselves in and don't come out until we've given them the word."

"That should work."

"Anything else?"

The other two were silent. "Let's do it," Recker said.

The three men got into Malloy's vehicle, with him behind the wheel. Recker and Haley hopped in the back seat, putting their masks on right away so nobody saw their faces going in. Malloy peeled out of the lot and turned to go to the hospital next door. He turned onto the hospital property and started driving the long winding road that led to the underground parking, the entrance of which was in back of the hospital. Malloy eventually stopped the car when he got to the booth that automatically dispensed the parking stubs since there was an officer stationed there to prevent anyone from going in. Being on Vincent's payroll, the officer immediately recognized Malloy. The officer looked at Malloy, then at the two masked men in the back seat, already being told of the plan.

"You guys really gonna do this?"

"Sure am," Malloy answered.

"Well, it's your funeral."

The officer raised the parking garage gate arm so the car could go through. Malloy drove through, finding an empty spot to park. They parked on the top floor since it was closest to the stairs that they'd have to breach in order to get into the hospital. The three men got out of the car, made sure all their gear was intact and ready to go, then walked over to three police officers that were guarding the steps. One of the officers shook hands with Malloy.

"Wish we were going in with you."

Malloy nodded. He wouldn't have minded the extra help. "Yeah. We all have our orders though."

"Yeah," the officer said, sounding a bit ticked off that

he wasn't getting in on the action. "Tell you what, send a few of them down this way and we'll take them out for you."

"Sounds like a plan. What about the door that leads in there? They got men on it?"

The officer shrugged. "Don't know for sure. It's a brown door, you know the ones, with the metal handle in the middle that you press down on to open. Can't see inside."

"You try to open it?" Recker said through his mask.

"Yeah, when we first got here. It was locked. No way to open it from our side. Locked on the inside."

Malloy looked at Recker. "We'll either have to break it down or blow it open."

"If we try and break it down, and it takes a little while, they'll know we're coming," Recker said.

"Yeah."

"If we just blow it open, we can still catch them by surprise."

"What if they have hostages by the door?" the officer asked.

"They wouldn't have hostages so close to an exit and risk them slipping away," Recker replied.

"Blow it open it is," Malloy said.

"You guys have any?" the officer asked.

Recker looked at the man, like he was crazy for even asking such a thing. He was never ill-prepared for any situation. "I got some in my bag."

Recker went back to Malloy's vehicle and removed a

small pack of explosives, just enough to blow the door open.

"So, who are these guys?" the officer asked, curious about the team going inside.

"Don't ask so many questions," Malloy replied. "The less you know the better."

Recker came back a minute later and went up the steps to inspect the door. He came back not long after that, with a sour expression on his face, not that anyone could see it.

"It's not gonna work," Recker said.

"Why?" Haley asked.

"There's no place for us to take cover from it. We'd have to stand all the way down the steps. That'll delay our entry for too long. The surprise element would be long gone by the time we get there."

"What about a battering ram?" Malloy asked.

"You got one?" Recker replied.

"In the trunk of my car."

"You always carry one with you?"

Malloy smiled. "Nah. Brought it along just for here. Never know what you might need."

Recker and Malloy walked back to his car so Recker could put his explosives away as Malloy grabbed the battering ram. They walked back to the main group, ready to go.

"This'll take me out of the fight for a minute," Malloy said. "Won't have my gun ready."

"Let the officer do it," Recker replied.

"Yeah, let me do it," the officer happily said.

Malloy handed the ram over to the officer. Recker made sure the officer knew exactly what he was doing.

"Listen, you ram that door, then you step aside so we can go through."

"Roger that," the officer said.

"After you ram it, make sure you get back quick in case the bullets come in hot and heavy."

"You got it."

Recker looked at each man. "You all ready."

"Let's go," Haley said.

The four men went over to the stairwell and walked up a couple steps until they got to the locked door. Before doing anything, the officer looked at the men to make sure they were ready. The team brought their rifles up, ready to aim and fire. Recker looked at the man and nodded.

"Before we go in," Malloy said. "Just to be clear, we're not taking prisoners, right?"

"Hell no," Recker answered.

"Just wanted to make sure."

"We take out whoever gets in our way. Seek and destroy."

15

The officer slammed the door with the battering ram, breaking the door wide open. He immediately jumped back so the team could go in, Recker first, then Haley and Malloy. As soon as Recker rushed through the door, he saw a man to his right, only a few feet away. The man was surprised by the door and brought his gun up, but Recker quickly mowed him down. As he dealt with him, there was another Scorpion to the left, somewhat disguised by the door opening. Just as the man pointed his gun at Recker's head, Haley jumped in, shooting him dead before he had the chance to pull the trigger. As Malloy came in, the other two stood there, looking down different hallways, aiming their rifles in case someone else appeared. Malloy looked down at the two dead bodies, a little disappointed there wasn't another one.

"Hey, you didn't leave one for me!"

"Don't worry," Recker said. "I'm sure there'll be plenty of chances for you."

"Which way?" Haley asked.

"It's a cinch we can't use the elevator. Gotta take the stairs."

"Which way's that?" Malloy asked.

"Over here."

Recker started running down the hallway, the others quickly following him, though they also kept looking over their shoulder to make sure they didn't get jumped from behind. Recker crouched down, then looked through the small piece of glass in the door to see if there were any men inside. Haley and Malloy watched his back, continuously looking for signs of trouble.

"We're good," Recker said, throwing open the door, as the three men went inside.

Almost immediately, they heard voices coming from somewhere above them. Recker put two fingers in the air, believing it to be two men talking from the sound of their voices. The three men slowly and quietly started walking up the steps, rifles aimed and ready to fire. As they rounded a corner, ready to go up the next flight of steps, Recker quickly stopped, the two men coming into range. Recker put his arm up to stop the others. Recker leaned his head forward to make sure he was assessing the situation properly. There were two men there, though their weapons were being held very loosely. They wouldn't have been much trouble. Recker put two fingers in the air again. Recker gave his friends a hand signal, letting them know he was about to go. Recker jumped out onto the platform and fired at the first man, easily dropping him. Just as the other man brought his rifle up, Haley and Malloy jumped out as well. They both fired simultaneously, killing the man before he was able to fire.

"Mine hit him first," Malloy said.

"No, it didn't," Haley said. "You're still trailing."

"Would you just let me have one to myself? Jeez."

Recker led the group up the steps and stood just outside of the second-floor hallway. He peered through the piece of glass in the door, observing a few more Scorpions.

"What do we do?" Haley asked. "Take them out on each floor?"

"That might mean it takes a while to get to Mia," Recker answered.

"If we go straight to the fifth floor though, it's a good chance they'll know we're here, which means the rest could come up and try to overpower us."

"I know. But each second we delay in getting Mia means she's not getting the care that she needs. I'd hate to think that something happens because we didn't get there soon enough."

"Understood."

"If you guys wanna start here, go floor by floor and take them out, I'll go right up to the fifth floor myself."

Haley shook his head. "Not how it works, brother. We either all go up and get her or we all wait here. There ain't no splitting up."

"I just don't want you guys to get into something you can't get out of."

"I knew what I signed up for coming in here. If we go up there and get surrounded because of it... it's just part of the deal. The idea was to come in and get Mia, not stay safe in my bed. If I was concerned about that, I would've stayed home. Whatever happens, I'm good with it."

Recker then looked to Malloy. "Don't bother looking at me," Malloy said "Everything he said goes for me too. Let's get her and do this."

"I just don't wanna get on Vincent's hit list if something happens to you."

Malloy laughed. "Hey, if none of us make it out, it's all good. You can't be killed twice, right?"

"All right, let's keep going."

"It's not gonna take them long to find these bodies and figure out we're here. Maybe we should hide them or something."

Recker took a quick look around, but there was no place they could take them that was within easy reach. "Doesn't matter. Even if we did that, they'll find out soon enough anyway if they see they're not at their stations or they're not responding on the radio. Best thing we can do is just get to the fifth floor as soon as possible."

The team continued going up the steps, though not as quickly as they would have liked. They had to assume there might have been guards at each floor of the stairs and didn't want to give themselves away by making the noises that running up the steps would make. Once they made their way up to the third floor, they saw the same situation. Two guards standing there, talking to each other, looking relaxed, and not expecting a confrontation.

Malloy tapped Recker on the shoulder, wanting to take the lead on this one. Recker nodded, letting Malloy go past him. Malloy poked his head around the corner, seeing the two men standing there, one of them with their leg resting against the wall. Malloy jumped out, shooting the man to his left first. Recker and Haley then jumped out behind Malloy, ready to take out the second man. Malloy beat them to it though. The man with his leg resting wasn't able to get himself ready in time, and Malloy drilled him with a hole right through his chest.

Malloy seemed thrilled with his work. "Ha, beat the both of you!"

"Nice," Recker said, going past him, and continuing their march up the stairs.

They slowly ascended the stairs until they reached the fourth floor. Recker poked his head out to observe the situation, just like he'd done on the previous few floors. He noticed two men standing there again. This time was different though. This time, the two guards actually seemed to be paying attention to their job and noticed a man in a black mask poking his head out.

"Cops!" one of the Scorpions shouted.

Both men brought their assault weapons up and started firing down the staircase. Recker and his friends immediately took a few steps back, trying to take cover amidst the hail of bullets that came flying at them. They all dropped to the ground, hoping nothing would hit them, as some of the bullets started to ricochet.

"Damn," Recker sighed, knowing their quiet assault

was now over. Everyone in the hospital would now know they were there.

As the three men continued to wait for an opportunity to strike, the two Scorpions weren't letting up. They just kept firing, not even caring that they didn't have an obvious target.

"They gotta stop sometime, don't they?" Malloy asked.

"One of us is gonna have to take the plunge," Haley replied.

"Wait until they slow up or change mag's," Recker said.

After what seemed like forever, the firing finally stopped. Recker rolled over on the ground, as his two friends jumped out, still on their feet. All three of them fired at nearly the same time, none of them quite knowing who shot who. All that really mattered though was the two Scorpions were now out of the way.

"You guys good?" Recker said, looking up. He noticed a small red spot on the arm of Malloy.

Malloy looked down at his arm. "Just a scratch. No big deal. I'm good."

"Chris?"

"I think I'm good," Haley answered, not really taking the time to check himself.

Recker got up to his knees, just in time to see the door that led to the hallway suddenly open. "Incoming!"

Recker dropped back down to the ground and saw a few armed men come out. He immediately started firing as Haley and Malloy also opened up. The first Scorpion that came through the door fell to the ground as the men behind him retreated back onto the third floor. The team stayed in their positions for a minute, waiting for more opponents to come through the door, though none seemed to be coming.

"We gotta move," Malloy said. "We can't stay here, or they'll start to box us in."

Recker knew he was right. Staying in the stairwell wasn't exactly good cover either. There was nowhere to hide and nowhere to go if they started to close in on them from both ends of the stairs.

"I just wanna make sure we don't take one in the back after we pass this floor," Recker said.

The de facto leader of the group with Billings incapacitated at the moment, Bill Cummins, was alerted to the fact that they had a new problem. The voice bellowed loudly over their radio's.

"We got a problem down here!"

Cummins angrily took the radio off his belt. "What?"

"We got intruders."

"Well, take care of it!"

"We already got seven men down."

"What?!"

"They've already taken out seven of us."

"Where are they?!"

"Stairwell. Level three."

"Cops?"

"I don't know. Don't think so."

"How many are there?"

"I'm not sure. Could be anywhere between two and five. Tough to tell."

Cummins tried to think for a minute before replying. He looked to his tough-looking, bald-headed friend, Maglio, for some answers and to bounce a few ideas off him.

"What are they doing?" Cummins asked.

"They're coming for us."

"I'm surprised. I didn't think the cops would break in so soon. Maybe we need to shoot a few more hostages to drive them back?"

Maglio shook his head. He seemed to be much more in tune with what was really going on. "They're not cops."

"How do you know?"

"Because cops wouldn't put all these people in danger by storming up the building. They would wait until it was a more advantageous position for them. They especially wouldn't do it with so few men. They'd have teams all over the place coordinating their hits to sync up with each other."

"So, who is it?"

"I dunno. Someone who doesn't like us for some reason probably."

"We'll take out a few of the hostages," Cummins said. "That should drive them back for a little while."

"That ain't gonna work. Whoever these people are, they're not cops, they already know about these hostages, they don't care. Taking some of these people out isn't gonna slow them down."

"Could be just a SWAT team."

"It ain't SWAT. I'm telling you now, these aren't cops. They wouldn't put these people in danger like that."

"So, what are we gonna do?"

"They're in the stairwell? Surround them. Box them off. Make them immobile."

Cummins nodded. "We'll come at them from all sides."

"That's the smart play."

Cummins grabbed hold of his radio again. "All teams, we got intruders in the stairwell. Between floors three and four. Block them off in the stairwell and crush the bastards. Keep one man at your current posts, everyone else, take these guys out."

For some reason, it didn't occur to Cummins that their opponents could hear everything he was saying on the radio. With three dead men not too far away from them, Recker and team intently listened to the communication over the radio. They knew exactly what they were planning.

"We gotta move," Haley said. "They're coming."

"We could just keep going up," Malloy said. "Keep marching on and hope we get there before the rest of the guys get here."

"We still got two more floors to go," Recker replied. "By the time we get to the fifth floor, they're gonna be ready for us. We gotta alternate course."

"But where to?"

Recker turned around and looked down the steps, then looked up. He didn't hear anyone coming yet, but he knew they were running out of time. He then looked at the door that led to the third floor.

"In there." Haley and Malloy both looked at him and saw Recker pointing to the door. Recker then looked back at them. "It's our best chance. Everyone's converging on this stairway. If we exit on that floor, there's a stairway on the other side of the floor, we can continue up on that side while everyone's over here."

Haley nodded, agreeing it was their best chance at the moment.

"There's no doubt they're gonna have more men on that floor already," Malloy said. "We're probably gonna have to fight our way to that other side."

"Good chance," Recker said.

"That might take away the surprise of making it to the other stairway."

"Might."

"Only other option we have is to stay here," Haley said. "And we know they're coming from both sides."

Malloy didn't have to think long to figure out staying put wasn't the better strategy. "Third floor it is."

16

Recker, Haley, and Malloy went up the couple steps to get to the third-floor platform. As the other two men stood guard, each aiming their rifles at opposing ends of the stairs, Recker brought his head up to the glass part of the door. He peeked in with one eye to try to get a view of what they were walking into, making sure most of his head wasn't made visible to become a target. After a minute, he took his head away to explain the situation.

"Mostly just a hallway," Recker said. "Looks like to the left is some type of desk. Might be a nurse's station or something. If there's anyone hiding, they're probably there."

"How far away?" Haley asked.

"Maybe twenty feet."

"You lead the way," Malloy said.

"Stay down, if they're there, they'll probably be shooting high."

Recker threw open the door, then rushed into the hallway and dove onto the floor. He made sure to make enough noise that he would draw the fire of whoever was waiting there for them. Two men jumped up from behind the desk and started shooting. Since they were focused on Recker, they weren't aware of Haley and Malloy coming through the door. They immediately picked up on the two Scorpions and instantly knocked them off, each of them taking one shot each to kill the men. Recker got back to his feet, and the three men huddled around, turning to see if there were any other immediate threats. It looked clear.

"Where is everybody?" Malloy asked, assuming there would be more activity going on.

They looked around, but there wasn't a sign of anyone. Staff, visitors, patients, not a person in sight.

"I figured there'd be people sitting on the floor or something."

"They probably locked themselves in their rooms," Recker replied.

"Should we check?"

"No. Doesn't really concern us at the moment. It's for the better anyway. Nobody to get in our way."

They quickly walked down the hallway, though not going too fast and possibly running into an ambush. They kept their guns pointed at every door as they walked past them. About halfway down the hall, they could hear one of the handles start to jiggle. Recker put his hand up to stop the team from going any further, as he kept his eyes focused on the door. A few seconds later the door opened up. Recker brought his gun up and aimed, ready to fire. He quickly ascertained the person wasn't a threat, as it appeared to be a patient or a visitor. It was an elderly woman, in her sixties. He wouldn't have put it past the Scorpions to have someone like that in their group, just to throw their opponents off and get the upper hand, but Recker could see that she wasn't armed. Her hands were well out in front of her.

"Are you the police?" she asked.

"Just get inside, ma'am," Recker replied. "There's still a bunch of them out here. Get inside and lock the door. We'll come around again when it's safe to come out, OK?"

The woman did as was requested and went inside. Recker heard the door lock again.

"Maybe we should give her a gun," Malloy said. "She can watch our backs in case anyone else comes down here and follows us."

"Yeah, nothing bad could happen there."

As they walked toward the end of the hallway, and the other staircase was in sight, the team could hear Jones' voice in their earpieces.

"How is it going?" Jones asked.

"Can't really talk now," Recker answered.

"You haven't checked in since you got there, at least give me something, so I don't worry out of my mind."

"We're in the hospital, have taken out nine of their guys so far."

"Are you on the fifth floor yet?"

"Third. We got diverted. We're trying to make our way up there now."

"OK. Just check in every now and then if you can."

"Will do."

The end of the hallway intersected with another one, which meant they'd have to cross some open space before they got to it. Haley and Malloy knelt down on opposite sides of Recker, peeking around both corners to protect him as he went across. They didn't see anyone. Recker started to run across when the door to the staircase suddenly opened. A man with a gun, presumably one of the Scorpions, stepped out and immediately started firing at Recker. One of the bullets stopped Recker right in his tracks, the force of the shot knocking him onto his back. Haley and Malloy rose up from their positions and returned fire. Haley went down as well. Malloy was able to drop the man before he did any more damage, though it looked like he'd caused enough as it was.

Malloy briefly looked down at his fallen friends, but then looked back toward the door, waiting, expecting more action to start happening any second. After a little bit of time went by, he assumed the man was acting alone. Malloy took another peek down all three hallways, then crossed over and opened the door to the stairs. He popped his head in but didn't see anyone else there. With the coast clear for the moment, he turned his attention back to his friends. He rushed over to their bodies, kneeling between the two of them. He put one hand on each of them to check their conditions.

"You OK?"

Haley sat up, holding his left shoulder. "Yeah, I'm all right."

"You hit?" Malloy observed some red spots on his arm, so he already knew that he was.

Haley held his shoulder, then started moving it around. "Nah, I'm good. Didn't go through. I think it just stunned me a little. I'll be fine."

They then turned their attention to Recker, whose eyes were still closed.

"Mike, you OK?" Malloy said, tapping his cheeks. He then checked for a pulse. He still had one.

"Mike?" Haley said, shaking his body slightly, hoping it would jar him back awake.

The two of them checked Recker's body for holes but didn't see any. At least there was no blood anywhere.

"Think he just got the wind knocked out of him or something," Malloy said. "Mike?"

A few seconds later, Recker opened his eyes. With the help of his friends, he slowly sat up. He groaned for a second while holding his chest.

"Whoever made these things sure knew what they were doing," Recker said. "Hope there's a special place in Heaven for them. They're a saint as far as I'm concerned."

"Well, if we get out of here, make sure you send him a special prayer of thanks," Malloy said. "Assuming he's dead and not with us anymore."

"Even if he ain't," Haley said.

"We gotta keep moving," Recker said.

"Sure you're good?" Malloy asked. "Need a few extra minutes?"

"I'm good. Don't worry about me. Mia's the one that can't afford any extra time."

Haley and Malloy helped their friend get back to his feet. Recker stood there for a second to make sure his balance was still OK. He nodded to let the others know he was still good to go.

"I'm good. Let's go."

With Haley leading the way this time, they crossed the hall and went through the door that led to the stairwell. As soon as they took a few steps, they could hear what sounded like a bunch of men quickly descending the stairs. They stayed put, ready to meet whatever was coming their way. They raised their rifles, aiming for a spot on the wall, waiting for a man to walk into their view. A few seconds later, a group of men came into their view. As soon as they did, Recker and company fired a round, killing the Scorpions out in front of the bunch. The ones behind them immediately opened fire, a hail of gunfire erupting, causing Recker's team to run for cover. They didn't want to get caught in a firefight in the stairwell, as it was too easy to get struck with a glancing bullet that could have been going anywhere.

Recker led the team back through the door and into the third-floor hallway. Just in time to see more Scorpions coming from the other end of the hallway, from the stairwell they'd previously been in. Both sides opened up, one of the Scorpions going down, but in the process splitting up Recker and Malloy from Haley, as they each took up opposite corners of the hall for cover. As everyone on both sides ducked for cover, Recker looked all around, not liking the situation they were now in.

"I think these hallways all intersect with each other," Recker said. "They'll be able to come up from behind us."

Recker took a few deep puffs of air as he tried to think of a way out of their situation.

"They're boxing us in," Malloy said. "They got us pinned down."

"As long as we can move, we're not done yet. Anybody notice how many guys were in that staircase?"

"No, couldn't tell," Haley said.

"Me neither," Malloy said. "Too much going on."

"You have something in mind?"

"Maybe," Recker answered. "Either we go back through that door and take our chances with whoever and how many people are on those stairs... or we go back where we came from and try the other steps again."

"Might work. If everyone thinks we're on this side and is pulling over here, we might have a small opening to make it up the other way."

"Not gonna be much of an opening," Malloy said.

"All we need is something," Recker said. "That's more than we got at the moment."

"I hear that."

Recker then looked at the door that led to the stairs. "It's only a matter of time before they come through that door."

"I'm surprised they haven't already."

"Chris, let's go back through these hallways and meet back up on the other side by the stairs."

"Split up?" Haley asked.

"I think we have to. You run across back to us and

you're gonna take fire from two spots. Whoever's behind that door and whoever's in that hallway."

"Roger that, let's do it."

Haley immediately took off down his end of the hallway, stopping once he got to the corner, surveying what was around it. Recker kept an eye on him as long as he could until he turned the corner.

Recker tapped Malloy on the shoulder. "Let's go."

The two of them went down their end of the hallway, keeping their guns out in front, ready to fire at a moment's notice. Malloy kept turning around, expecting someone to come up behind them.

"Maybe we should duck in a room somewhere," Malloy said. "They'll spend a lot of time looking for us. Won't know where we went."

"Then we'll be pinning ourselves down without anywhere to go."

"Yeah, you're right."

"Plus, it's still the same problem. Too much time."

"Yeah, forget I said it."

Recker chuckled. "Already did."

They walked down another thirty feet before they both instinctively turned around at the same time. It might have also had something to do with hearing something hitting a wall, possibly part of a gun. In any case, Recker and Malloy turned around and fell to the ground at the same time, all while simultaneously firing their gun. The two Scorpions behind them got some shots in, all of which missed, though they wouldn't have if Recker and Malloy had stayed upright. Dropping to the ground saved them from a certain death. In the process, they were able to put two more notches on their guns. They got up just in time to see another Scorpion coming at them. Recker and Malloy both drilled the man at the same time, their bullets entering the man's body only an inch away from each other. They continued walking down their path, completely circuiting their side of the third floor, until they came back to where they began. They saw the three dead bodies behind the nurse's station from when they first came in.

"Chris, where are you?" Recker asked.

"One more corner to go."

A few seconds later, they saw Haley stick his head around the last corner.

"I see you," Recker said. "Should be clear."

Recker and Malloy moved up past the desk and knelt on one knee, keeping their eyes peeled. Haley started running toward their position. As he was just about there, Recker noticed some movement behind him.

"Drop!" Recker shouted.

Haley immediately hit the deck, Recker and Malloy instantly firing over the top of him, shooting at the Scorpion who was coming up behind Haley. After his friends had stopped shooting, Haley rolled over onto his back and looked at the dead body behind him.

"Thanks," Haley said.

"Let's get the hell off this floor," Recker replied. He then looked to the door that led to the stairs that they were originally on. "I'll take lead on the steps. You guys keep an eye back there."

Haley and Malloy jumped to the middle of the hall-way, in plain view, on one knee, ready to shoot whatever came into their sights. Recker then rushed over to the door and opened it, finding it empty except for a few dead bodies that they had previously taken care of.

"We're clear!" Recker said, rushing through the door.

Haley stood up and followed his partner, then Malloy. They started moving up the steps more quickly this time. The Scorpions already knew they were there. There was no use trying to hide it or move slowly now. Now, they just had to get ready for whatever was going to meet them next.

17

The team came around the corner, expecting to see some action as they approached the fourth floor. They were pleasantly surprised to not see anyone standing there. Instead of moving on, though, they stayed in place for a few moments, analyzing the situation. Malloy looked in favor of going, not liking standing still for any period of time.

"C'mon, why aren't you going?"

Recker looked around. "It doesn't feel right."

"What do you mean? Why not?"

"There've been men stationed at each floor. Now all of a sudden there's not. Breaking away from pattern is always a cause for concern. Usually means something's up."

"They were probably part of the group that met us on the third floor," Malloy replied.

"Maybe." Recker then looked at his usual partner to get his reaction. "What do you think?"

Haley took a second to take in the situation, his eyes darting all around. "Yeah, I'm with you. It doesn't feel right."

"That's just you guys being paranoid," Malloy said. "C'mon, we gotta go. I'll take the lead."

"No, wait," Recker said.

Malloy didn't listen and kept going up the stairs. He passed by the door that led to the fourth-floor hallway. Recker and Haley followed him, though they kept a little distance between them. As soon as Malloy turned the corner to keep going up, the door opened, a couple Scorpions showing themselves as they fired off several rounds at him. Malloy turned around to return fire but had already been hit and fell to the ground. Before the two men noticed Recker and Haley coming up, they had already been fired upon. Recker and Haley took the men out easily and continued slowly moving up the steps, waiting for someone else to jump out at them. As they stood on the fourth-floor platform, with the door open, they could see a lot of people sitting around on the floors inside. There sounded like a lot of low whispering going on, and some crying, as the hostages weren't sure what was going on.

"Mike?" Haley said.

"Yeah, I see them."

"What do you wanna do?"

Recker turned his head to look at Malloy, who was sitting up with his back against the wall, holding his leg.

"Ask them if anyone else is on the floor," Recker said.

As Haley went inside, Recker went over to Malloy to check on his condition. Malloy laughed as he came over.

"Guess I should've listened to you, huh?"

"Sometimes I know what I'm talking about," Recker answered. "How you feel?"

"Like I've been shot. Freaking careless."

As they talked, Haley went inside the floor, first looking for signs of further trouble. With nothing that presented itself immediately, he looked down at a bunch of hostages, mostly hospital staff, who were all silently looking up at him, wondering what was going on.

"Are there any others here?" Haley asked.

"Are you the police?" a doctor spoke up.

"Are there any other armed men here?!"

"Uh, no, no, I don't think so. I think it was just the two. There were more, but they left a few minutes ago to go somewhere else I guess."

Haley looked around, seeing what he estimated to be close to a hundred people sitting in the halls. "All right, he's what I need you to do. You need to get all these people into a room and lock the doors, you understand?"

The doctor and several other doctors and nurses around him stood up. "We will."

"There's still a bunch of dangerous people walking around and until we know they're gone, don't come out of your rooms until you're told to, you understand?"

"We do."

"All right, go."

Haley stood there for a few seconds, watching as the people chaotically scrambled around to find a room to duck into. In less than a minute, all of the people had disappeared. With that taken care of, Haley walked back into the stairwell. He saw Recker butting a bandage around Malloy's thigh to stop the bleeding.

"All right, I told them all to find a room and stay in it."

Recker looked up at him. "Good."

Haley then looked at Malloy. "What about him?"

"I don't know. Think you're good enough to move or you wanna stay put somewhere?"

"Just get me to my feet and I'll be fine," Malloy answered.

"You sure? We can put you somewhere and come back and get you after we get Mia."

Malloy shook his head. "You're not getting rid of me that easy."

"I just wanna make sure you'll be able to keep up and that you're not gonna be an easy target."

Malloy stuck his arms out. "Just help me to my feet and I'll be fine."

Recker and Haley reached down and helped pull Malloy back to his feet. Malloy grimaced and limped as he took a couple of steps, but it was nothing that he couldn't push through. His partners looked at him, not sure if he could continue, but Malloy was adamant about not being left behind. He was still in the fight.

"Seems similar to that last time we got shot, huh?" Malloy said. "Remember that building?"

"Yeah, except that time we were going down," Recker replied. "This time we're going up."

"Going up steps is gonna be hard with that leg," Haley

said.

"We only got one more floor to go," Malloy said. "I'll get there."

Recker nodded at Haley for him to take point. He wanted to stay back with Malloy to make sure he didn't drag behind. Recker wanted to make sure that Malloy kept up, mostly because he didn't want him so far behind that he risked getting surrounded or ambushed and killed. Haley left the others behind and went up to the next floor alone. He wasn't charging in blind though, and still took his time to get up the steps, trying to do it as quietly as possible. As he got to the fifth floor, he peered around the edge of the steps, looking up at the platform, and was surprised to once again not see anyone there. He kept his position and waited for the others to catch up to him.

"We're clear here," Haley said, just wanting to let them know before they got there.

Recker and Malloy began moving, Malloy going first, as Recker stayed behind to make sure they didn't have any surprise visitors sneaking up on them. He was in a good amount of pain, and moving definitely wasn't easy on him, but Malloy somehow was able to keep his leg moving. Haley kept his eyes peeled, surveying the situation until the other two got to his position.

"Anything?" Recker asked.

"Nothing," Haley replied. "It's a cinch they're in there though."

"No question about it."

"Just a matter of how many."

"It'd be nice if we could somehow get in there by surprise."

"Not happening. There's no way."

"I'll tell you what we could have done," Malloy said. "Since we had the fourth floor cleared off, two of us could've snuck around and came up the other way. While they expect us to come in the front, we come in from the back too. That would have caught them by surprise."

"Might still be able to do it," Haley said.

Recker quickly nixed the idea though. "It's too late for that now. Might've worked if we did it right away. All we've done now is allow them more time to catch up. Besides, we already know they had people in that other stairwell. Might just be trading one problem for another."

Cummins got on his radio. "What's the status down there?!"

"They're off the third floor. Think they just passed the fourth too."

"Hurry up and get up here!" Cummins looked at Maglio. "What do these guys want?"

Maglio looked at the hostages on the floor for a second. "Think it's pretty easy. They either want to finish Tommy or they want one of these people."

Cummins took a quick look around at the people sitting on the floor. "Nobody would be dumb enough to come in here just for one of these people."

"Must be Tommy then. I guess they wanna make sure

he doesn't get out of this hospital alive. If these guys come up here, maybe we should get these people out of sight?"

"Why?"

Maglio shrugged. "I dunno. That way they don't get in the line of fire."

"Screw these people. I don't care if they're in the line of fire or not. If they get hit, so be it."

"OK."

"Did you take the phones off those nurses you brought up here?"

"No, I didn't even check them, why?"

"What if one of them is the reason these guys are here?! Why would you not check them?"

"Didn't think it was necessary."

"I told everyone before we got here that I wanted all phones confiscated so there was no outside contact with anybody!"

"Didn't think it was important," Maglio replied.

Cummins looked perturbed and sighed, angry that his orders weren't fully carried out. "Where are they at?"

Maglio looked around, then pointed at two of them. "Those ones over there. Then the one you shot is in that room."

Cummins went over to the nurses and demanded their phones, which they promptly handed over to him. They were locked, so he asked for their pin numbers so he could login and check them. Once they did, he checked their message and call history. There was nothing there since the Scorpions took over the hospital. He tossed them to the side on the floor.

"It's not them," Cummins said. "Where's the other chick?"

Maglio pointed to the room Mia was in. "In there."

Cummins barged into the room, seeing the doctor and nurse checking on her. "She got a phone on her?"

The doctor reached into his pocket and removed Mia's phone, knowing that's what they were looking for. "Not that I know of."

Cummins went over to Mia and started combing through every pocket he could find, not having the slightest concern over her well-being. The doctor put his hands on Mia's arms to hold her still and also slid the phone under her back.

"A little more care please," the doctor said.

Cummins finished checking Mia's pockets. He took a step back and looked at the doctor. "How about you? She give the phone to you?"

The doctor shook his head. "She handed me nothing."

"Put your hands up."

The doctor did as he was asked and threw his arms up. Cummins then came over to him and checked all of his pockets as well. Pants, shirt, doctor's coat, there was nothing. Cummins, a little unhappy, then started walking toward the door to leave.

"May we please have our equipment so we can operate on this woman?" the doctor asked.

"Why, is she gonna die?"

"She may if we don't get this bullet out."

"Let her," Cummins said, walking out the door.

18

The team stood there for a minute, trying to think of their next move. They knew they had almost no time to stay there any longer than that.

"We're gonna have to move," Malloy said. "They're gonna be coming up behind us any second now."

Recker still didn't move. He was almost paralyzed. He knew Mia was not too far away from him now. And he wanted to make sure nothing he did put her in further jeopardy. What seemed like a million thoughts were going through his head, trying to analyze every step they could make or take, and what the response to that action would be. What they could really use was some type of diversion.

"What are you thinking?" Haley asked, knowing it was something.

"We need some type of edge," Recker answered.

"Can't argue there. Whatcha got in mind?"

Recker instinctively put his hand on one of his pockets, feeling the edge of his phone. He then pulled it out and sent a text message to the doctor.

"Do you know how many of them are on your floor?"

"Cover behind me for a minute," Recker said, wanting to get an answer before proceeding. A few seconds later, he got it.

"I believe six or eight."

"I got an idea," Recker said.

"What is it?" Haley replied.

"We're gonna give ourselves up."

"What?"

"Just listen."

"Give this phone to whoever's in charge. I'm calling in a second."

The doctor didn't question the orders at all and immediately walked into the hall, holding the phone out in front of him. Cummins noticed his strange behavior and walked over to him.

"What's this?"

"I believe this is what you were looking for?" the doctor answered. "Someone sent a text saying to give it to you and expect a call."

Cummins looked at him strangely, not sure what was going on. Five seconds later, the phone started ringing. Cummins gently took the phone from the doctor's hand, almost like he was apprehensive about it.

"Who is this?" Cummins asked.

"I honestly have no idea," the doctor replied. He then retreated back into the room to continue checking on Mia.

Cummins put the phone up to his ear. "Who is this?"

"That's not important," Recker said.

"Who are you and what do you want?"

"I told you that's not important. I wanna make a deal with you?"

"What kind of deal?"

"We'll give ourselves up, no questions asked, if you let the hostages you have on your floor go."

"You're crazy if you think I'm gonna do that."

"You'd be crazy if you didn't," Recker said. "You've already lost ten men. How many more are you comfortable losing?"

"As many as it takes. We've still got enough to get you, eventually. You're not gonna be able to take us all down."

"Maybe not, but we can significantly weaken your defenses for when the police eventually come through."

"I'm not making any deals," Cummins repeated defiantly.

"Suit yourself. But I'll make sure you and Billings never leave this place if you don't."

Cummins cleared his throat and thought for a second. "What is it exactly that you wanna do?"

"I wanna see all the hostages you have on that floor gone. You let them go down the steps and me and my five men will step out and hand over our guns."

"Why would you do that?"

"Because I understand you've already hurt innocent people in there. I wanna make sure that doesn't continue."

"I think you're trying to pull something on me."

"I'm not. Just wanna make a deal that benefits everybody."

"You're just gonna give yourself up for everybody, just like that?"

"Yes."

"Why would you do that?" Cummins asked again, not understanding the concept of someone sacrificing themselves for the greater good. It was something that he would never do.

"Is it a deal?"

Cummins waited a few seconds before responding. "Nah, no, no way. You're gonna pull something. I'll let those people go and all it'll do is give you a better target to shoot at."

"Fine, I'll give you something better than my word."

"What's that?"

"I'll give you me," Recker replied.

Haley tapped Recker on the arm, wondering what he was doing. Recker just glanced at him and shook him off though. He knew what he was doing.

"How's that gonna work?" Cummins asked.

"I'll walk through the door. I'll be unarmed. As soon as you see me, you let the hostages walk out of there. Once they do, the rest of my men will walk through the doors unarmed as well."

"With the hostages gone, how do I know they won't come in shooting?"

"Well, I'll still be standing there unarmed. You can keep a gun on me. If they start shooting, I'm obviously a dead man. Sounds like a winning proposition for you."

Cummins started pacing up and down the hallway, scratching his head as he thought about the offer. It almost sounded too good to be true. In the back of his mind, he knew it had to be some type of trap. It had to be. Nobody would just give themselves up like that, he thought.

"All right, give me a minute to think about it."

"Better call off your men first," Recker said. "Because if I run into any of them before you accept this offer, then it's off the table, and you'll have lost another five men in the process."

"OK, OK, just hold on."

"Call me back at this number."

A few seconds later, they could hear Cummins talking on the radio, that they still didn't know Recker could hear.

"All Scorpions," Cummins said. "Hold your current positioning. Do not move, do not engage anyone until further instructions."

Recker, Haley, and Malloy all looked at each other. "Well that gave us a few extra minutes," Haley said. "But what's the point?"

Recker then explained his plan. "The point is, we need to get the hostages out of there before we go barging in."

"Why?" Malloy asked. "What difference does it make?"

"Because the last thing we need is to go in there shooting and having a hundred people going all over the place in chaos."

"Yeah, that would make things more chaotic," Haley said.

"At least if we get the hostages off the floor, we'll have clear targets."

"They gotta know this is some type of trap," Malloy said.

"They're desperate," Recker replied. "They need Billings and they're gonna do whatever it takes to make that happen. They're not in a position where they can just sit and wait for more of their men to get knocked off. With every man they lose, they lose the advantage they initially had coming in here. They need us to stop. They should be willing to do just about anything to do that."

"Hope you're right."

"Me too."

"But you said we'll come in through that other stairwell," Haley said. "I don't know if we'll be able to make it over there. Like you said, they might have people in there already."

"I just said that to give them somewhere else to look," Recker said. "If I tell them you're coming in from another spot, even if that changes their eyes for a second or two, that might give us all the time we need for you guys to come in and knock a few of them off before they realize what's going on."

The others nodded, feeling like it was as good a plan as any. They weren't sure if it would work, or go down as Recker hoped it would, but they really had no other alternatives. The only other alternative was to play games for another hour and try to sneak their way in, maybe through a ceiling or a vent or something, but that would just be taking too much time. Time they didn't have.

"What if they just stall?" Malloy said. "What if they have no plans to answer you either way? They just wanna buy time for their guys to get into a better position and smoke us out."

Recker pointed to the radio that he swiped from one of the dead Scorpions. "I think we'd have heard something if they were planning a setup."

Another minute went by. Then Recker's phone started ringing. It was Cummins.

"OK. I agree to your terms. I'll let these hostages go as soon as you and your men step in."

"That's not the deal," Recker said. "I step in, you let the hostages go. Once they're gone, the rest of my men will show up too."

"Fine. Do it."

"OK. I'll be in in a minute. Don't be shooting." They hung up, and Recker looked at his partners. "It's go time."

"How we working this?" Haley asked.

"I'll go in, then when all the hostages are off, I'll say, 'They should be coming through that door.' That'll be your cue to come in."

"OK."

"Come in hot and heavy. Don't worry about where I am. Just start shooting."

"Will do."

"You're not really going in empty-handed, are you?" Malloy asked. "What if they shoot you before we get in there?"

"I always have a backup."

Recker then walked up the steps to the fifth-floor platform, Haley and Malloy right behind him, though they made sure they remained out of sight. Recker peeked his head through the glass and saw several men standing there, waiting for his arrival, though they were off in the distance. They weren't standing too close in case he came in shooting. Recker pulled open the door, immediately seeing dozens of hospital staff sitting there on the floor. They all looked up at him, hopeful that he was the one who was going to get them out of their situation. Recker then looked at the Scorpions, easily identifiable with the guns in their hands. He counted four right off the bat. Two in the middle of the hall, and one to his right, one to his left.

"Who's the guy I talked to?" Recker asked.

"I am," Cummins replied, standing in the middle of the hallway.

"You wanna release them?"

"Drop your gun first."

Recker tossed his rifle on the ground.

"Take off your mask."

"After they leave," Recker said.

"Turn around so I can see you don't have anything else on you."

Recker turned completely around, hoping they wouldn't notice the gun inside the back of his pants. His shirt came down over the top of it, concealing it completely. But even if they spotted it, he still had another gun strapped to his leg underneath his pants.

"The hostages?" Recker asked.

"All right, everyone can go."

The hostages weren't sure what was happening and were slow getting up, not sure they could actually move.

"C'mon, get out of here!" Cummins yelled.

"Hostages this way," Recker said, pointing to the door he just came from. He kept his arms up and stood to the side as they started filtering out.

As the hostages went through the door, they were immediately greeted by Haley and Malloy on the steps. They just kept waving to the people to continue going down the steps. Once all the hostages were out of sight, Haley and Malloy snuck closer to the door, ducking just behind it as they waited for their cue.

"Take off your mask," Cummins repeated, since the hostages were gone.

Recker pulled his mask off, holding the hood in his hand. "That everyone?"

"It's everyone you're gonna get. There's still a few more people in these other rooms, but they're staying put for now." Cummins studied the man's face, hoping he would recognize it, but he didn't. "Now, bring in the rest of your men."

"Before I do that, what exactly is your plan here? Why are you doing this?"

"We're waiting on our friend until he's well enough to be moved. They said it'll be a few hours. That's why we're doing this."

"Doesn't seem very logical. You can tell you don't do this type of thing very often. You did everything all wrong."

"Listen, man, I don't need to take any of your crap. Now, you gonna bring your men in here? Because if you don't, I'll just shoot you right now and deal with them later."

"Calm down, calm down, I'll bring them in." Recker then pointed to the other door at the far end of the hall. "They should be coming in that door over there."

"That's our cue," Haley said.

"Light them up," Malloy replied.

19

Just as several of the Scorpions turned around to look at the other end of the hallway, Haley and Malloy burst through the door. Haley stood tall, while Malloy dove onto the floor, not wanting to put too much trust into his leg at the moment. They each immediately took aim at the Scorpions directly ahead of them. As soon as the gunfire started, Recker dove onto the floor and reached around to his back for his pistol, nailing the man that was to his immediate right. Haley then picked off the one to Recker's left.

The remaining Scorpions retreated to the end of the hall, ducking into a couple of the rooms, ducking their heads out and taking a few random shots. Recker took a quick look around, and, not seeing Mia, knew she had to be in one of those rooms ahead of them. While Malloy crawled on the floor to a better position, Haley reached down and found Recker's rifle, then tossed it over to him.

Recker put his mask back on, just in case there was anyone else lingering around, they wouldn't have a chance to see his face. Recker and Haley then each found a corner to get behind. Worried that they would be coming up behind him, Recker knew a way to stop that.

"Jimmy, you keep your eyes on that door," Recker said, pointing to the steps they just came from. "Just focus on that and take out whoever comes in. We'll focus on these jokers."

"You got it."

Recker and Haley exchanged fire briefly with the remaining Scorpions on the floor. As one of the Scorpions stuck his head out to take another shot, Haley carefully aimed at him, hitting the man square in the head, dropping him instantly.

"Think there's two left," Recker said.

Cummins and Maglio knew it was getting too hot in there and they had to leave the scene. They'd have to figure out Billings' situation at another time. Their plan had unraveled, and they lost control. They came out of their rooms quickly, rapidly firing in the direction of their opponents. They just wanted to get them ducking for cover to aid in their escape. It worked. Recker and Haley kept their bodies tucked behind the corner of the wall, making sure even the smallest piece of them wasn't exposed. After the bullets stopped, Recker and Haley peeked around the corner, seeing the two last Scorpions fleeing toward the other stairwell.

"Let them go," Recker said.

He didn't want to keep shooting in the event there

were more innocent people on the floor. If a bullet got away from them, or if their targets shot back and missed, and the shots entered a room and hit someone, killing them in the process, it just wasn't worth it. It was better to just let them go. Besides, now his thoughts were turning to Mia again. He needed to find her.

"Start checking doors," Recker said. "Keep your guard up in case any of them got left behind."

"Right."

Recker took the right side of the hallway, while Haley took the left. Malloy still kept his eyes planted firmly on the door, waiting for another round of action. The first doors the team checked on both sides were empty. The next two were the same thing. Once they got to the next set of doors, Haley pushed the door open, seeing a doctor and nurse standing over someone. He rushed in to see who it was.

Haley grabbed Mia's hand. "We're here."

Mia groggily looked up at him and smiled.

"Mike! She's here!"

Recker darted into the room, trading places with Haley.

"I'll keep a lookout," Haley said, exiting the room, continuing to check the other doors.

Mia smiled upon seeing Recker's eyes. "I knew you'd come."

"Nothing would stop that." Recker looked over at the doctor, wondering about her status. "What does she need?"

"She needs to get into an operating room, and she needs it now."

"Can you do it?"

"Yes, but we need to move quickly. She should have been in that operating room an hour ago."

"OK. You wheel her to where she needs to go. We'll provide cover for you."

"Are they still out there?" the doctor asked.

"I think we've cleared them from this floor, but we can't be sure yet. We'll accompany you to the operating room."

"I could use an extra pair of hands."

Haley appeared in the frame of the door. "You've got them." He finished checking the other rooms. There were another five nurses stashed in there, taking care of patients.

"Let's go," Recker said.

The doctor and nurse helped put Mia on a bed and wheeled her out of the room. Recker and Haley walked alongside her as they walked down the hallway to get to the operating room.

"Jimmy, you good over there?"

"Ten-four," Malloy answered. "How's the missus?"

"Alive. We're taking her to the operating room. Just keep your position."

"Roger that."

"Chris, take up position at the other stairwell and make sure nobody comes through."

"Will do," Haley said, running over to it.

Once they got to the operating room, several of the

nurses took Mia in, while the doctor and a few other nurses got scrubbed up. Recker held her hand as they waited for the doctor to come back in.

"You're gonna be OK," Recker said.

"I'm glad you're here," Mia replied.

"You're gonna be fine. I promise."

"If I don't make it, I want you to know that I love you. And that you're the best thing that ever happened to me."

"Don't talk like that. You're gonna be fine."

"Just in case I don't, I want you to promise me something."

"Anything."

"Promise me you'll move on and find someone else. That you won't let what happened to you the last time happen again. Don't close yourself off."

Recker smiled, trying hard not to drop any tears. "I won't have to worry about it. Because you're not going anywhere."

"Just promise me."

"I promise."

A few minutes later the doctor and other nurses entered the room.

"I'm afraid you'll have to step back," the doctor said.

"That's fine," Recker replied. "I'm actually gonna wait just outside the door to make sure we get no unauthorized visitors. Do what you have to do."

"I'll let you know when we're finished."

"About how long should it take?"

"About an hour. Rough estimate."

"Then after that?"

"Let's just take it one step at a time so I can see what the damage is."

"I'll be outside."

Recker took one last look at Mia, then walked out of the room to take up standing guard. He should have given her a kiss before leaving, he thought. What if that was their last moment spent together? He quickly shook those thoughts out of his mind, refusing to believe that was going to be it. Mia was strong. She was a fighter. Something like this wouldn't be her downfall. She was going to beat it. Recker believed that.

"We gotta make sure we hold off for about an hour," Recker told his partners.

"Sounds good to me," Malloy replied.

"No problem here," Haley said. "How's she doing?"

"Don't know yet," Recker answered.

"She'll pull through."

"I hope so."

"She will. By the way, while I was checking those other rooms, I found Billings."

"Which room?" Malloy asked.

"516."

"If they still want him, they're gonna make another try for him."

"I think we can pretty safely assume that they will," Recker said. "At least one more."

"That reminds me, how much longer you think the cops are gonna hold off for? If they heard the gunshots, they must be getting pretty antsy right about now."

"Yeah. I would think we'll be seeing them pretty soon. At least a SWAT team or something."

They all stayed in their spots for another ten minutes, without any further issues, or a sign of the Scorpions still being around. Recker was getting antsy though. Whether it was just Mia's situation on his mind, or anticipating another assault by the Scorpions, or assuming the police were coming in soon, or maybe all of the above, he started to pace around a little bit. Not very far from the door though, just in case there was an update about Mia.

"We got movement over here," Malloy said.

"What you got?" Recker replied.

"Not sure yet. I can see shadows moving around in the stairwell through that glass part of the door."

"See anything on your side, Chris?"

"Negative."

"All right, stay sharp. If they start coming in, let me know and I'll come back you up."

"You got it," Malloy said.

About two minutes went by. Recker assumed it was the Scorpions, getting ready to make another push. But it also could have been hostages who were making their way down the building if they had escaped or were let go. He didn't really believe that though. He expected to receive a call for help any minute. And two minutes after that, he got it.

Malloy stuck to his spot, sitting there on one knee, patiently waiting for the door to fully open. It moved open a crack, as if someone was trying to sneak their way in. Malloy wanted to be positive about who it was before firing at them. It kept moving open slowly and Malloy readied himself.

"Got someone coming in," Malloy said. "Slowly."

"Scorpions?" Recker asked.

"Can't tell yet."

The door opened just enough now for someone to sneak in, and one of the Scorpions tried crawling in to avoid being detected. It obviously didn't work with Malloy watching the door. Malloy instantly fired, killing the man before he was able to stand up.

"One down," Malloy said.

A second later, the door opened quickly, several Scorpions rushing in. Malloy immediately engaged, the two sides swapping bullets.

"Three more just came in!" Malloy shouted.

As soon as he heard the words, Recker immediately left his post and started running down the hall to assist. "I'm on my way."

"Want me to lend a hand?" Haley asked.

"No, stay there," Recker replied. "Just in case they try to do a double."

Malloy crawled over to a different position so as not to be in the line of fire so much. He also hoped to move the Scorpions position, so they would have their backs turned as Recker approached. Malloy, while waiting for Recker to arrive, lay down on his stomach and reached around a desk, aiming for one of the men's legs. He fired, hitting a man in the shin, instantly dropping him to the ground. Once the man's full body was in view, Malloy fired a couple more rounds through the man's torso.

"Two left," Malloy said.

Recker came down the hallway to the left of the door, seeing the backs of two men who were shooting at Malloy. He raised his rifle and took aim. His first shot went right through the back of the man's head. As the Scorpion to the right turned around, Recker fired again, this time the bullet going through the man's chest. Once the man dropped to the ground, Recker updated the situation.

"None left." Recker continued looking, not initially seeing Malloy at first. "Jimmy, you OK?"

He then saw Malloy's head poke up above the desk. He put his thumb up in the air. "Good to go."

"Good. I'm heading back to my post."

"I'll let you know if I need anything."

"Hopefully, that was it," Haley said. "Hope they got the message that it's over."

"Maybe," Recker said. "But I doubt it. I don't think we're out of the woods yet."

20

It was only a few minutes later that Haley started to report a similar issue on his side. He saw the door move a crack, though it didn't appear to move any further than that. It actually looked like someone was about to go in, then changed their mind and retreated.

"What do you think?" Haley asked.

"I think they're coming," Recker replied. "I think they might be testing things to see how well each side is guarded. They tried the other side first. Now they'll try here."

"Let's hope they don't decide to do both doors at once."

"That might be next."

Feeling like they were about to get an assault on Haley's side soon, Recker left his position once again and headed down to where his friend was. About a minute after Recker got there, the door flew open, several Scorpions bursting through. On Malloy's side, the Scorpions tried to sneak their way in. That obviously didn't work. This time, they were going in full blast, trying to force their way in with power.

Recker and Haley were ready for them though. Haley shot the first man through in the chest, Recker took care of the man behind the first guy, also hitting him in the chest. A third man came in, Haley also dropping him. Then a fourth one came through, with Recker finishing it up. Four bodies piled up on the floor, almost directly on top of one another.

"Think that's it?" Haley asked.

"I dunno. We'll find out in a minute."

A few more minutes went by without any other issues. Instead of just waiting there for another round, Haley got an idea.

"Cover me?"

"What are you doing?" Recker asked.

"You'll see."

Haley went over to the door and grabbed each of the dead bodies and dragged them closer to the door, putting them right up against it. He made sure each of the bodies were on top of each other, leaning their weight against the door to prevent it from opening easily. Recker smiled once he was finished.

"Why make it easy for them?" Haley said.

"That's a good call."

"They won't be sneaking in again on this side."

Recker then looked down the hall at Malloy's position. "Maybe we should do the same down there."

"Wouldn't hurt."

Recker went back down the hall to Malloy's side, dragging a couple dead bodies with him. Along with the bodies that were already lying around there that tried to come in, they had five people to stack up in front of the door.

"That should hold them a little while," Recker said.

"They gotta be close to bailing," Malloy said.

"I agree," Haley replied. "They're taking too many hits. I lost count, but they gotta be down about twenty guys now. That's a major hit to anybody. They can't just keep coming full bore like this. At some point, they gotta retreat, live to fight another day."

"Retreating isn't something these guys are used to," Recker said.

"Hey, everyone does it sooner or later."

Recker stood there thinking, trying to add up all the Scorpions that were killed. In the chaos of all the action, it was tough to remember every single piece of it, but he suspected that Haley's number was pretty close to being accurate.

"I guess how long they plan on staying depends on how many they brought to begin with," Recker said. "If they brought eighty guys, they still have sixty left. Still a lot of firepower."

"They can't have everyone here," Haley replied. "That's just taking so much to chance. I mean, they're willing to wipe out their entire organization over this? That's just not smart business."

"I think I'll side with Chris on this one," Malloy said.

"Having a little understanding of how these organizations work, they wouldn't bring in everybody. Just in case they ran into a problem, they still have guys on the outside. They could still recruit, bring in new members."

"With a hospital this size, you still need a lot of men to cover everything," Recker said.

"Yeah, but you know you can't cover everything. Maybe you put a couple men at each floor, a man or two inside the floors, plus a few on the ground floor to cover the entrances to hold off the police... I figure they brought in around forty. Maybe fifty at the high end."

"If that's true then we took out about half of them."

"Either way, they can't be feeling too comfortable about now," Haley said. "They gotta be thinking about escaping at some point."

Their discussion was soon interrupted as a call came in to Recker's phone. It was Jones. Recker walked down the hallway again to get to where the operating room was.

"Yeah? A little busy here."

"I'm well aware," Jones said. "I thought I should point out that you are about to have a new problem."

"And what's that?"

"The police."

"What about them?"

"They're coming in."

"How do you know?"

"Watching news coverage, reading reports, everything. They're coming in. And they're coming in now."

"Well, it'll probably work out better for us that they do."

"How do you figure?" Jones asked.

"Well, by our calculations, we think we've taken out about half of them now. We think they had about forty to start with."

"Have you gotten to Mia yet?"

"Yes. She's in surgery now. We're guarding the fifth floor right now. We drove the Scorpions off the floor for the moment. So, she's being operated on, but we also discovered that Billings is on this floor. This whole thing was about getting Billings, but they couldn't move him yet. Something about how he couldn't be moved for a few hours."

"That makes sense. What's Mia's prognosis?"

"I don't know yet. Probably have another forty minutes or so."

"She'll make it. I know she will."

"Yeah."

"I know that's where your main focus is at the moment and rightfully so, but you have to start thinking about leaving."

"I'm not going anywhere."

"Michael, the whole point of this was to get Mia and get her help. You've done that. There's nothing else you can do there. If the police are coming into the building, the Scorpions are no longer a concern for you. The police will round up whoever's left assuming they haven't fled the building already."

"I can't leave her. Not now."

"I'm not trying to argue or say that you're inherently

wrong or that I don't understand your feelings, but you can't do anything for Mia if the police lock you up."

"Don't forget I still have a get out of jail free card in my back pocket."

"I was hoping we wouldn't need to use that unless it was absolutely necessary."

"It's necessary now," Recker said.

"What about Chris and Malloy?"

"Chris has got a card too."

"What about Malloy? He went in there with the sole intention of helping you."

"He knew the risks before he came in."

"That doesn't mean you shouldn't do all you can to protect the people that willingly went in there with you, knowingly putting themselves in danger for the sole purpose of helping you."

"It's a cruel game we play. We all know that."

"What about Mia?" Jones asked.

"What about her?"

"You're gonna blow her cover in the process."

"What do you mean?"

"Once the police take you into custody, you don't think they're going to put two and two together and figure out your relationship with her? First of all, the police will start putting pressure on her to reveal what she knows about you. Second, once it's out that you two are together, every criminal in the city is going to look to use that to their advantage. You want another Jeremiah situation on your hands?"

Recker sighed, not really wanting to hear any of it. Not

that he could necessarily deny any of what he was saying was wrong. He just didn't want to hear it.

"So, what do you want me to do? Just fly out of here without knowing what's happening with her?"

"That's not at all what I'm suggesting," Jones answered.

"Then what are you saying?"

"I'm saying you need to make yourself scarce when the police arrive. When Mia gets out of surgery, do you really think she wants to hear the news that you're in a jail somewhere instead of being there by her side?"

"I guess not," Recker solemnly said.

"Then just trust me. Make sure you're not there when the police get there. Just do something to disappear for the time being."

Recker sighed, taking Jones' words in, becoming more receptive to them. "OK. I gotta talk to Chris and Malloy first and figure something out then."

"OK. Just let me know what you decide."

After getting through with Jones, Recker immediately sought input from the other members of his team. He touched his earpiece to connect with the others.

"Guys, I just heard from David. Looks like the police are about to enter the building."

"Is that good or bad?" Haley asked.

"Could be either depending on what we wanna do."

"Just trading one problem for another," Malloy said. "That'll drive out the Scorpions. But now we gotta deal with the cops."

"Jimmy, how many are friendly to you?"

"Not enough where we could just stroll right out of here and walk past them. There's a few, but too many more who'd be asking questions."

"I was afraid of that."

"How much time you figure we have?" Haley asked.

"I dunno. Five, ten minutes. Can't imagine it'll be too much more than that. Guess it'll depend on the Scorpions and if they run into them, and if they just give up or make a fight out of it. They'll run into them before they get to us."

"I assume we're not taking on the police when they get here?"

"No, but I don't wanna just lay down for them either," Recker answered. "Especially with Mia in there, there's gonna be too many questions. And she deserves to have someone there with her when she gets out of there."

"I agree. What's the solution then?"

"I don't know. Haven't got one yet."

"I might have something," Malloy said.

"What you got?"

"We blend in."

"We're in riot and tactical gear, how do you propose we do that?" Recker asked.

"There's a lot of rooms on this floor. I'm sure there's some extra uniforms or something."

"We don't exactly look like doctors."

"We get changed, stash our equipment, then walk out with everyone else."

"Or we could just take everything off," Haley said. "We got regular clothes on underneath. We could just say we were visitors. We could go lock ourselves in a room somewhere and wait it out."

"Yeah, I guess that might work too," Recker said. "Either of those plans seem like it's our best option. Which will it be?"

"I say we just say we're patients."

"Yeah, I can go along with that," Malloy said. "If you wanna do it the boring way."

"All right, I guess that's what we're gonna do then. Chris, were there empty rooms when you checked?"

"Yeah, a couple. What are we gonna do about Malloy's leg?"

"I'll just say I was one of the unlucky ones the Scorpions tried to make an example out of. Unless I can bandage it up and find a new pair of pants without blood on it, then I can just limp my way out."

"With your record, I'm not sure they'd buy that you weren't involved somehow."

"We'll just have to give it a shot and see what happens."

"How are we gonna know when they actually get here?" Haley asked. "I'd prefer not to shut everything down, assuming they're getting here pronto, only to have them take their time and have the Scorpions take one last run at things and catch us unprepared."

"Yeah, that's a problem," Recker said. He pulled out his phone again and called Jones. "Hey, do you know if the cops are in yet?"

"They are in the building."

"You're sure?"

"Definitely."

"OK, thanks."

"What are you planning to do?" Jones asked.

"Wing it."

Jones put his phone down. "That doesn't exactly inspire confidence," he said to himself.

"They're in," Recker told his partners.

"Yeah, but how long?" Haley asked.

"Can't be long."

"I say we take a chance and grab a room real quick," Malloy said.

"I'm inclined to agree. Hey, what about your cop friend in the garage?"

"That's a good idea. I'll give him a call."

Recker and Haley patiently waited as Malloy called the police officer that assisted them in the parking garage. About a minute later, Malloy gave them the news.

"Hey, looks like we got less than five minutes."

"They're on the way up?" Recker asked.

"They're clearing the third floor now."

"What about the Scorpions?"

"They said they've arrested five of them so far. The rest are probably in the wind."

"How could the rest get out of the building?" Haley asked.

"They had an escape plan before they got in here," Recker answered. "They knew how they were getting out."

"Yeah. Well, guess we need to get out of sight."

"You guys find a room. I'm gonna check on Mia first."

"Will do."

As the other two moved from their positions to find an empty room, Recker knocked on the door to the operating room. He didn't wait for someone to come, peeking inside instead. Once his entire body was in the room, he motioned for one of the nurses to come over.

"Is everything OK?" the nurse asked.

"Yeah. I'm gonna have to go, but the threat is over, so you guys will be safe. The police are almost here. Should be here in a few minutes."

"The police? Wait, aren't you the police?"

"No. But you guys are in the clear now, OK?"

"Thank you."

"How is she doing?" Recker asked.

"She's doing well. She's going to make it."

Recker could feel a gigantic weight lift off his shoulders. "How much longer?"

"It'll probably be a half hour at least."

"But she's going to pull through? You're sure?"

"I'm ninety-five percent certain she'll make it. The biggest issue she had was the amount of blood she lost. But she's doing fine. She's a fighter."

"Seems that way."

"Do you know her?"

"No. But I know she has a boyfriend," Recker said. "I'll get word out to him somehow that she's here."

"That would be great."

"Mike, where are you?" Haley asked. "Time's running short."

"I'm on the way." Recker took another quick look at Mia, then left the room. "Where are you?"

"I'm in room 525. Malloy's not here yet."

"Malloy? You coming?"

"Yeah," Malloy replied. "I'll be there in a minute. Just gotta finish something."

"Finish what?"

"Don't worry about it."

Malloy limped along the hallway, picking up one of the guns that were lying beside the dead body of one of the Scorpions. He marched along until he got to room 516. He went inside, pushing the door open slowly, in case there were any Scorpions still in there alongside their friend. It was empty though. Not even a hospital staffer. It was better that way for what Malloy intended. He walked over to the bed that Billings was lying on. The Scorpion leader was sleeping, not having any idea the danger that was coming his way. Malloy crept up beside him, then raised the gun he just stole, pointing it at Billings' chest. He unleashed three rounds, all of which entered Billings' chest and remained there. Malloy stayed put for a moment until Billings' heart monitor stopped. It was just one long continuous beep. He was gone.

Malloy then turned around and walked out of the room, taking a look around to see if they had any visitors yet. With it clear for now, he walked back over to the dead Scorpion and dropped the gun back down on the floor, next to the body. He turned, ready to find where his friends were.

"What room you guys in?" Malloy asked.

"525," Haley answered.

Malloy went down the hall and turned to his left,

finding the door on his left-hand side. Once in, he was immediately grilled about what he was doing.

"Where were you?" Recker asked.

"Finishing something."

"Finishing what?"

"Finishing what we started," Malloy answered.

"What's that mean?"

"It means nobody has to worry about something like this happening again."

Recker and Haley looked at each other, believing they knew what he was referring to.

"You killed him?" Recker asked.

"Is anyone gonna shed a tear over it?"

It wasn't that they were necessarily upset over Billings being dead. It was the fact that he wasn't armed and wasn't a threat. That's really what bothered Recker and Haley more than anything. Malloy was right, they wouldn't shed any tears over it. It was just killing an unarmed and defenseless man was stepping over the line as far as they were concerned. But then again, Malloy operated under a different line than they did.

"Hope it doesn't come back to you," Recker said.

"It won't. I used the gun of one of the dead guys out there. It'll look like they came in here to kill him."

They started getting undressed, taking off all their gear. They put everything, including their guns, inside the closet in the room. They went through a couple of the drawers in the room, finding a few basic medical supplies, basically some bandages to wrap Malloy's wound. Once they were finished, they sat down on the bed, waiting for the next domino to fall.

"What's the next move?" Haley asked.

Recker quickly responded. "Only thing we have to do now... is wait."

21

A fter being in the room for about ten minutes, they heard a knock on the door.

"Police, open up!"

Recker went over to the door, trying to play the part of a hostage. "How do I know it's really the police?"

"Just open the door and I can show you."

"Maybe you're one of the bad guys trying to trick us."

Haley and Malloy had a laugh on the bed. "You tell them," Haley said.

"Please, sir, just open the door."

"I don't know."

"We can kick it in if we have to. Just save us the trouble and open the door."

"Well, OK."

Recker opened the door slightly, just enough to see a police officer standing there. He was in full uniform, so there was no doubt about his claim, unless the Scorpions switched tactics and started impersonating the men in blue. But that was doubtful.

"The threat's over, sir," the officer said. "Anybody else in there with you?"

Recker opened the door all the way, allowing the officer to look inside and see his friends.

"All those guys are gone?" Haley asked.

"They are?"

"Everyone here OK?"

"Yeah, we're good. We were visiting our relatives here and these guys just started shooting so we locked ourselves in here."

"You did the right thing."

"I'm gonna keep checking these other rooms here, but did you guys notice anyone else fighting against the guys that took over the hospital?"

"We heard some shooting out there," Recker answered. "But we didn't see who it was. We just hunkered down behind the bed there and prayed for the best."

"Well, it's over now."

"Thankfully."

"Are we able to leave yet?" Haley asked.

"Not just yet," the officer replied. "There will be some detectives and other officers coming in soon to get a statement from everybody."

"How long will that take? This has been such an ordeal. We just wanna go home soon."

"I understand. It won't take too long. Someone should be along in a few minutes. Just wait here. Won't be long."

"Thank you."

The officer then went down the hall until he got to the next room. Recker turned around and shrugged at his friends.

"Guess we gotta wait. Hope we don't get someone in here who recognizes me."

"It's taken care of," Malloy said.

"What? How?"

"You'll see."

A minute later, another officer appeared in the door. It was the same one that was in the parking garage that let them in the building.

"About time you got here," Malloy said.

"Got here as quick as I could," the officer replied. "It's a madhouse out there." The officer looked at Recker, recognizing his face immediately. "You're him. The Silencer. I didn't recognize you before with the mask on, but you're him, aren't you?"

Recker stood there silently, not answering.

Malloy replied for him. "Is there a problem with that?"

The officer looked a little nervous. "No. No problem."

"Good. Let's just get us out of here then."

The officer then took a bag off his shoulder and handed it to Recker.

"What's this for?" Recker asked.

"Guns," Malloy replied. "Figured we could sneak them out instead of leaving them here."

"Oh."

Recker went over to the closet and started putting their weapons in the bag. Then he stuffed all their clothes on top of them. He then came back to the middle of the room, where the officer reached for the bag.

"I'll take that."

Recker looked over to Malloy, who nodded. With his approval, Recker let the cop take the bag, who slung it over his shoulder.

"You hurt?" the officer asked, noticing the blood on Malloy's leg.

"It's nothing. I'll be fine."

"You want me to get a doctor in here?"

"No. I just wanna get out of this place as quickly as possible. Vincent will take me to one of his doctors. Keep it off the books."

"How are we getting out of here?" Haley asked.

"We're gonna walk," Malloy answered.

"How?"

"Just follow me," the officer said. "I'll get you all out of here without a problem."

"How are you gonna do that?"

"There's thousands of people in here. After we get everybody's statement, names, and addresses, we're letting everyone go who doesn't have some kind of business here. Hospital staff and patients mostly. With all the bodies lying around, there's crime scenes everywhere. They need to start processing them."

"They're just gonna let a parade of people go down those stairwells with dead bodies all over the place?" Recker asked.

"No. Elevators."

"That's gonna take a while."

"Yeah, well, as soon as we're done interviewing people, we're to escort them to the elevators. There's a couple on every floor, so assuming people are done being questioned at different times, hopefully it won't be backed up too much. It is what it is, can't really help it too much."

"Wait, I thought the elevators were disabled?" Haley asked.

"They were. They're back up and running again."

"So, are you supposed to be talking to us?" Recker asked.

"Like I said, there's thousands of people in here," the officer said. "They're not gonna notice if three guys walked out of here without giving a statement."

"What about cameras?" Haley asked.

"Cameras are still offline. From what I hear it'll be another hour or two before they're back online."

"Sounds like you got it all worked out."

"Only if we move now."

"What are we waiting for then?" Recker asked. "Let's move out."

"You need help?" Haley asked, tapping Malloy on the arm.

"No, I'll be OK. Last thing we need is for people to see an injured man getting helped out of here. Brings too much attention. I'll grin and bear it."

"You guys got everything?" the officer asked.

Recker looked at the others, who all nodded they were ready. "We're good. Let's roll."

Led by the police officer, Recker, Haley, and Malloy walked out of the room and down the hall. They passed by several other officers and detectives, none of whom paid a lick of attention to them. They were all way too busy in their own right, interviewing people themselves. Though Malloy still had some pain in his leg, he managed to walk to the elevator almost without a limp. They were the first ones there at the elevator since everyone else was still being questioned. Once inside, Haley and Malloy each took a deep breath, feeling like they were almost out of it. But once those elevator doors closed, Recker could only feel like he was abandoning the love of his life. The whole point of this mission was to come in and get her, and even though she was now out of danger, and was going to pull through surgery just fine, he still felt like he failed. Mia was going to come out of surgery, and he wasn't going to be there for her. Recker wasn't even sure when he would be able to come back. It was a certainty that the police would be there for a while examining the crime scenes. And even when that was done, they might decide to leave a few officers there just in case. Would he be able to walk back in without going through some type of security? There were a lot of police officers that knew his face. He probably wouldn't be able to take the chance of coming back if the police were still there.

With the elevators running again, the team didn't have to worry about being spotted again, as the elevator opened up right at the parking garage level.

"Would've been nice if we could've just ridden that right up to the fifth floor to begin with," Haley said.

"Tell me about it," Malloy replied.

The officer handed Recker the bag, and he slung it

over his shoulder as the three men started walking through the garage to get back to Malloy's car. Malloy stopped and looked back at the officer to give him a final message before they left.

"Thanks for the help. Vincent will want to give you a little extra bonus for your efforts today."

The officer nodded. "Thank you."

Malloy walked back to the others to catch up with them, but he started limping a little more.

"Think the pain's finally starting to hit me," Malloy said.

"Probably 'cause the adrenaline rush is wearing off," Recker replied.

"Yeah, probably so."

Recker and Haley each grabbed one side of Malloy and put his arms around their shoulders, as they lifted him off the ground, so he didn't have to put any more weight on his injured leg. Once at the car, they put Malloy in the back seat, so he had a little more room to stretch his leg out. With everyone settled, Recker got in the driver's seat, and calmly drove out of the parking garage. There was still another police officer stationed there, but he was only preventing people from coming in. He didn't pay much attention to anyone coming out. He was told if someone was leaving, they'd already been vetted and questioned.

The team drove off the hospital property and back to the parking lot next to it. They got out of the car and Haley started rooting through the bag to take out their equipment.

"Well, it's been fun," Malloy said.

"You gonna be OK?" Recker asked.

"Yeah, I'll be fine."

"I mean to drive."

"I'll make it."

Even though he was sure Malloy would be able to manage all right, Recker still felt a little bad about just casting him off like that.

"I'll tell you what, why don't I drive you back to Vincent, then he can take you to his doctor from there."

"You don't have to do that," Malloy said.

"I know I don't have to. I just wanna make sure you don't get a severe pain in your leg and you cramp up, then swerve to the side of the road and kill somebody."

"How will you get back?" Haley asked.

"You can just follow me there. I'll drive him there, drop him off, then hitch a ride back with you."

"Sounds like a plan."

"You good with it?"

Malloy smiled. "You really take the good Samaritan bit a little too far sometimes."

"Maybe."

"But I won't argue with it. Thanks."

They got back in their respective cars and drove out of the lot, Haley following Recker.

"Looks like we made it after all, huh?" Malloy said.

Recker sighed, still not happy at the cost. "Yeah. Looks like we made it."

22

Once they were on the road for a few minutes, Recker called Vincent so he knew to be expecting them.

"How did the mission go?" Vincent asked.

"Not as smooth as I hoped it would," Recker answered. "But I can't say it was a failure either."

"Your lady friend, how is she?"

"She's gonna make it. We got her into surgery in time."

"I'm glad to hear it."

"Thanks again for helping out. We couldn't have done it without you."

"Sure you could have," Vincent said. "You would have found another way, I know you. Maybe it would have taken a little longer, but you would have found something else. When it comes to you against an immovable building, I'm still taking you."

Recker laughed. "Maybe. Still, it probably worked out better this way."

"I'm happy it worked out. Everyone make it out in one piece I gather?"

"Well, Jimmy took one in the leg. He's gonna need to see one of your doctors."

"Is it bad?"

"Not too bad. He'll be off his feet for a few days, but he'll live. He's not losing a leg or anything."

"Not yet, at least," Malloy said with a laugh.

"Well, thankfully it's not too bad."

"I'm bringing Malloy over to the warehouse if you wanna meet us there."

"Absolutely, I can be there in a few minutes. Now that I know all the main players made it out safely, how did the rest of the assignment go?"

"I think we took out around twenty of them," Recker replied. "Can't say for sure, lost count after a certain point, but it was around there."

"I guess that counts as a good day's work."

"It was costly for them."

"Losing twenty men is never an easy proposition, no matter how many you still have left."

"Even besides that," Recker said. "They lost Billings too."

"What?"

"Billings is dead."

"Oh? How did that happen?"

"Jimmy took the initiative to take him out before we left."

Vincent hesitated before replying, hoping the job wasn't sloppily done. "How was it handled?"

"Before the cops arrived, he used one of the Scorpions guns, killed him, then dropped the gun back down."

"So, it won't come back to you guys?"

"Shouldn't. If they do ballistics on it, they'll find the gun used belonged to one of their own."

"Well done."

"What this means from here on out is anyone's guess," Recker said.

"As far as The Scorpions?"

"Yeah, no telling how they're gonna react now. Billings is dead, the hospital takeover failed, they could go in a bunch of different ways from here."

"Only time will tell."

"I know you weren't ready to deal with them yet. Hopefully, this won't come back to you at all."

"If it does, then we'll deal with it," Vincent said. "It'll certainly be easier to deal with them with sixty members than eighty."

"Assuming they don't recruit more."

"As I said, we'll deal with it. If it does come back to me, or the next guy I deal with is not as willing to make a deal as Billings was, can I count on you to help exterminate them?"

Recker didn't even have to think about it. Vincent helped get him into the hospital. As far as Recker was concerned, the question didn't even need to be asked. One of the Scorpions shot Mia without reason. That was not something Recker was going to forgive or forget. There would be payback for it.

"You got it," Recker said. "Whatever is necessary."

"Good. I'll see you at the warehouse."

"See you there."

After putting his phone down, Recker looked at his passenger, seeing Malloy holding his leg. His facial expression indicated he was in a fair amount of pain.

"How you holding up?" Recker asked.

"Getting shot sucks."

"Can't argue there."

"How many times has it been for you?"

"Uh, I forget. Three? Maybe four? That doesn't count the times a bulletproof vest saved me."

"Yeah. Ever think about going into a safer line of work?" Malloy asked.

"No, not really. What else would I do?"

"I dunno. Banker?" Malloy laughed at the thought of Recker working in a bank. "That'd be quite a sight."

"The world's not ready for that."

"I never asked you before, but you worked for the CIA, didn't you?"

Recker was a little taken back by the question, catching him off guard. "What makes you think that?"

"The things you're able to do. The way you talk. Everything about you screams government agent. You were, weren't you?"

Recker thought for a second before replying, thinking about whether he really wanted to answer. "Yes. I was."

"What happened? Why'd you leave?"

"The decision was made for me."

"They let you go?"

"Uh, something like that. They tried to kill me."

"What? Really? The CIA?"

"Yeah. I was engaged to be married at the time. The person in charge of the program I was assigned to, decided I had become a security risk. So, they tried to terminate me."

"Well, I can obviously see they failed."

"They still looking for you?"

"No. The person who ordered the hit on me has since been removed. Whoever's in charge now recognized the issue and has put me back on the good list, so to speak."

"So, you're in the clear?"

"For now."

"So that woman, was that Mia?"

"No," Recker answered. "Her name was Carrie."

"What happened to her?"

"She was killed. They took her out at the same time they tried to kill me."

"Sorry to hear it."

"Yeah. What about your past? How'd you come to where you are now?"

Malloy looked out the window, remembering exactly how he got to this point. "This is where I was always going to end up."

"How so?"

"My mother died when I was young. I was probably five or six at the time. So, my father raised me. He wasn't a great dad, but I guess he did the best he could. He was always in some kind of trouble. He was like a small-time criminal, doing any small job that came his way. Breaking into cars, robbing houses, pick-pocketing, you know, whatever opportunity came his way."

"Just you?"

"Yeah, I was an only child thankfully. It'd been even rougher if another kid had to deal with all that nonsense. He was a drinker. Actually, he was an alcoholic. Ever since I could remember, I can't ever think of a day when he wasn't smashed by the time I went to bed."

"That's rough."

"Yeah, I mean, we made it work, I guess. Whenever there was an event at school, I always had to make up an excuse as to why my drunk father could never be there."

"You got through it OK?"

"Yeah. I don't know how, but I did. There were no baseball games or father and son trips or anything like that. It was just school, homework, watch your father drink himself into a drunken stupor, then go to bed and do it all over again the next day."

"Still talk to him?"

"No, he died," Malloy said. "Ironically, it was the day after I graduated from high school. He was coming home to take me out to dinner to celebrate. He was driving drunk, slammed right into a telephone pole, killed him instantly. It's funny, he hadn't taken me out to dinner in probably five years before that. Then the one time he was planning to actually do something with me... it's funny how life works sometimes."

"Yeah. Think things would have turned out differently for you had you had a normal childhood?"

"I dunno. Maybe. Maybe not. I'm not gonna be one of those people who blames what I've become on my parents or having a rough childhood. Everybody's got problems. People just deal with them in different ways. Everyone has choices to make, no matter what has happened to you in the past. But the choices I've made are mine. Nobody else's. I'm not gonna say I was driven to this. I could've done things differently if I wanted to. I just chose not to."

"So, how'd you end up with Vincent?"

"It was completely by accident. I don't remember how old I was. Probably around twenty or so. I was working in this warehouse and Vincent came in. I think he was working on some kind of deal. Anyway, it was about fifteen years ago, and he'd just risen to power, taking control of the northeast. For some reason, the deal went sideways, and people started shooting at each other. Everyone started taking cover. Vincent somehow ended up near my position."

"The start of a beautiful friendship."

"Yeah, well, anyway, one of the people shooting came around and had the drop on him. He was about to shoot him right in front of me. I saw the whole thing. So, I jumped out and started hitting the guy. I wound up dropping him, knocking him out."

"So, you left with Vincent right there?"

"No, him and the boys he had with him hurried up and escaped. He never forgot me though. He came back to that warehouse a few days later, wanting to thank me for what I did for him. He put a few hundred bucks in my pocket and asked if I wanted to make more money working for him."

"So you did?"

"Yeah."

"Did you know what he was doing?" Recker asked.

"Yeah, basically. He pretty much told me what I'd be doing. I started at the bottom doing a lot of low-level deals. He didn't hand me anything. But he knew he could always count on me."

"That's never changed."

"Took me about six, seven years to get to where I am now."

"Ever think about striking out on your own? Starting your own group?"

"Maybe it's crossed my mind a time or two," Malloy answered. "But never for very long. I'm happy with where I'm at, what I'm doing, and who I'm working for. I have some things that I'm very good at. To do what Vincent does, to last as long as he has, you have to sometimes do things differently. I'm not sure that's something I'd ever want to do or be interested in. Besides, I like where I am."

"Makes sense."

"What about you? Planning on staying in Philly forever?"

Recker shrugged. "Who knows? I honestly don't make plans that far ahead."

"I hear that."

"Besides, for the next little while, all my focus is going to be on the Scorpions. That might take some time."

"Why were you so focused on getting rid of them, anyway?" Malloy asked.

"It's actually a pretty simple answer. They're bad people who are capable of doing bad things. The longer they're here, the more work I'll have to do."

"And it's as simple as that?"

"It's as simple as that. Speaking of plans... what was your reasoning for taking out Billings back there?"

"I've got a simple answer of my own."

"Which is?"

"It was a good opportunity."

"But he was going to jail anyway," Recker said. "Why bother?"

"I don't want the Scorpions here either. They're bad for our business. Vincent's willing to wait and see how things shake out. I'm not as patient as he is. I'm much more of a strike while the iron's hot type of guy. Billings was obviously high up in their food chain. Even if he went to jail, at some point, he'd be back out and we'd have to deal with him again. Now we don't have to."

"And it's as simple as that?"

Malloy smiled. "It's as simple as that."

Once they finally got to the warehouse, they saw Vincent waiting in front of it, standing by his car. There were several more of his men stationed all around, just to make sure that Recker hadn't been followed by the Scorpions. Recker got out of the car and helped Malloy get into Vincent's vehicle. After a brief conversation, Recker grabbed his and Haley's gear out of Malloy's car. He then got back into Haley's car and they drove off, soon followed by Vincent, who went in a different direction to get Malloy to one of his doctors.

"Where you wanna go?" Haley asked.

"Let's get back to the office."

"What about Mia?"

"I'm gonna have to figure out a way to get in there."

"I could always go and check on her."

Recker tapped Haley on the leg, appreciating the gesture. "She'd like that. But somehow, I gotta find a way to see her myself. I can't just leave her there alone."

"We'll figure out something."

"Until then, we need to start working."

"On what?" Haley asked.

"We have to go hunting."

"For?"

"Some piece of crap opened up and put some lead into a beautiful, innocent person. I'm not gonna let them get away with that."

"You want the guy that pulled the trigger?"

"Oh, I want him in the worst way."

Recker's mind went back to the way he felt in trying to track down Agent 17. Hatred consumed him for taking away the woman he loved at that time. He was feeling it again, even though the circumstances were a little different, and Mia had pulled through.

"I don't care who he is. Whoever it is... they are going to pay."

23

Jones was still monitoring the situation at the hospital by the time Recker and Haley got back to the office. As they walked in the door, Jones came over to greet them, happy to see them back in one piece. He still looked them over, making sure they didn't have any holes in them that they neglected to report.

"How was Malloy?" Jones asked.

"He'll live," Recker answered. "It's nothing he won't recover from. He'll be off his feet for a week probably, but that's about it."

"Well, that's a good thing."

"You still been monitoring the hospital?"

"Of course?"

"Anything new?"

"Police are still processing the scene."

"What about victims?" Haley asked. "Anybody else other than what we know?"

"No, thank goodness. The only bodies that have been marked as deceased are known Scorpions."

"What about other casualties?" Recker asked.

"Two. One was Mia, as we know. The other was a visitor who apparently mouthed off at the beginning of the siege. He was shot in the leg but will make a full recovery. He's not in danger."

"Good."

"What's the chatter so far?" Haley asked. "What are they saying about us? If anything?"

"Right now, it's a big blur from what I can tell. Nobody seems to know or have any good theories about what happened, which is a good thing from our perspective. The prevailing opinion so far is that there happened to be a group of well-skilled people in the building at the time who decided to strike back."

"That's a pretty weak theory," Recker said.

"Maybe so," Jones said. "But it's the best one they have at the moment and the one they're going with. With the building surrounded at the time and all entrances and exits blocked off, they're saying it was impossible for someone to come in from the outside."

"Unless you happen to know a cop who's not quite on the up-and-up who'll let you in."

"Yes, well, let's hope they don't come to that conclusion as well. Speaking of which, is it possible they will find out about what that officer did?"

"I would think it's unlikely. I think he just said that if anyone asked that he'd say he broke the door open before the rest of the team got there, thinking he heard a hostage in danger."

"You think they will buy that?" Jones asked.

"With everything else going on there, you really think they'll doubt it?"

"Maybe not."

"He'll be fine. They have too much else to worry about."

Jones sat back down at his computer and started typing away. Recker went over to the big screen monitor on the wall.

"David, put up the known Scorpions on here."

Jones immediately brought the pictures of the group on the screen. "Why, what are you looking for?"

"We'll have to start crossing some of these guys off."

"As soon as I got final confirmation on the names of the bodies."

"Hey, what about Billings?" Haley asked. "Any blow-back on him?"

Jones sighed, still not liking the fact that he was killed in the manner in which he was. "Not that I can tell at this point."

"There won't be," Recker said.

"How can you be so sure?"

"Because Billings was killed with a gun that belonged to one of the Scorpions. Once they do ballistics, they'll find that out."

"They won't buy that they went into that hospital to kill him," Jones said.

"Maybe not initially, but they'll come around to that point of view."

"Why do you think so?"

"I think the official report will wind up saying that the Scorpions initially raided the building with the intention of freeing Billings. When that wasn't possible, they decided to take his life instead of letting him go to jail and possibly risk him turning evidence and giving the cops a lot of sensitive info."

"I think that's flimsy," Jones said. "Do you really think they would believe that?"

"What other option is there? They're bad guys, David. People in that line of work turn on each other all the time. It's not exactly unprecedented."

"Well, that is true. It just seems to me that would be a bit of a stretch."

"Considering he was shot with a gun of one of their own, what other evidence would they have to prove otherwise?"

Jones nodded, knowing he was correct. "No, you are right. It just seems... I don't know. The whole thing is a mess."

"It certainly is that."

Recker looked at the pictures on the screen, feeling the hate burn inside him with each face that he looked at. There were a couple faces that he recognized already, as he remembered shooting them at the hospital. But he knew somewhere on that screen was the no-good bastard that shot Mia. As he looked back, he should have tried to question someone to see who the person was who pulled the trigger. But he knew that wasn't the most pressing issue at the time when he was in the hospital. Besides, he fully intended to kill everyone on the floor anyway, making it a moot point. And it still might have turned out that he got the guy already, anyway. He didn't know for a fact that one of the men that escaped was actually the trigger man.

"I need to get back in there and see her," Recker said.

"I'm afraid that's not possible at the moment," Jones replied.

"I don't want to hear that. She's lying in a hospital bed recovering from a gunshot, I need to be there with her."

"Michael, listen to what I am saying. I am not telling you no because I don't think it's a good idea, though I really don't think it is, I'm telling you it's not possible because the police are not allowing anyone inside the building who is not authorized to be there right now. At least until they get the crime scenes cleaned up."

"Which means what?"

"Only people who are legitimately working at that hospital are allowed to be in that building. They are not even allowing visitors into the building at this point."

"For how long?"

"From what I can gather, they are going to revisit the situation tomorrow and make the call then as to whether they open it up again for visitors."

"They're still taking patients?"

"Yes, and don't get any ideas, because I won't allow you to injure yourself just to get in there."

"Not even what I was thinking of," Recker said.

"Pardon me for not exactly believing you. I know how you are. You are somehow going to find a way in that building."

"Well, you're right about that."

"With Billings dead, they shouldn't have too tight a grip on things," Haley said. "They'll probably just have a few guys stationed at entrances, watching, things like that, just to make sure there's no problem."

"Very well could be possible," Jones said. "Let's just wait until tomorrow and see how it all plays out before you start figuring out a way to enter in some unusual way."

"I wasn't even thinking about breaking in," Recker said.

"Then what did you have in mind?"

"Going in the front door like everybody else."

Jones looked at him with a slight level of distrust. He didn't quite like the sound of that. "Right through the front door?"

"Yep." Recker went over to one of the other cabinets and took out their disguise kit. He placed it down at the desk and looked at Jones. "Right through the front door."

Disguising themselves wasn't something Recker and Haley did often. When they did, throwing a baseball hat on was usually enough. But every few months they had a job where a little more finesse was needed. Put on some facial hair, maybe a scar or two, and voila, they were a different person. It was something they learned in the CIA, though neither of them usually much cared for such theatrics, either then or now. But sometimes it was unavoidable, and they needed to don those types of disguises. As far as Recker was concerned, this was one of those times.

"You got any problems with that?"

Jones shook his head. He knew how important Mia was to Recker, and to all of them for that matter. Seeing how she was and visiting her while she was stuck in a hospital bed, was something that needed to happen.

"I'll just be happy when all of this is behind us," Jones said.

"That might take a while."

"Why?"

"Scorpions are still out there," Recker answered. "We might have taken a good chunk of them out, but they still got some numbers."

"Maybe they will take this as a sign and split and go somewhere else."

"I think there's close to a zero percent chance of that happening. Especially after what else I've got planned."

Jones stopped typing, perplexed by his partner's words. He looked at him with a confused expression on his face. "What do you mean? What other plans do you have?"

"I'm gonna find out who shot Mia and I'm gonna make them pay the price for that."

"Michael, that's not what we're about here. We're about protecting the innocent. We're not about personal retribution and revenge."

"You're not. I am."

"We've been through this before."

"I know, and you don't have to tell me about it, I've lived it."

"Everything's fresh in your mind, you're still charged up. Just let it lie for a while, so you calm down and look at things with a new perspective."

"I don't need a new perspective," Recker said. "Calm, angry, relaxed, mad, it doesn't matter one bit. I'm gonna take them out."

"Take them out for the right reasons. Because it's the only way, to save a life, because it's the right thing to do... not because you're angry."

"I'll do what I feel like I have to do."

"So, what is the purpose of this visit for Mia? To actually be with her and comfort her and love her, to let her know you're there for her in her time of need... or to pump her for information so you can go on this vendetta of yours?"

"Do you really need to ask that question?"

"I didn't think I did, but maybe I do."

"Nothing is more important to me than her."

"I would hope not," Jones said. "Do you really think she would approve of you going out there, trying to gun down the man that shot her?"

"That's really an irrelevant question."

"Why?"

"Because she doesn't approve of anything we do to begin with. She'd rather me quit this whole thing altogether. So that really means nothing."

They continued talking for a few more minutes, but Recker had enough by that point and finally walked out of the office. He really didn't want to argue about anything. His mind was made up about what he was going to do, and he didn't want or need anyone's permission to do it. Haley walked over to the window and looked out, seeing Recker get in his car and drive off.

"He just left," Haley said.

"He just needs some time to cool down," Jones replied. "He'll be back."

"I can't really say I blame him."

"Neither do I. I just want him to act rationally instead of on emotions. Reacting on anger is what gets people killed. Especially when we're dealing with people on the level of the Scorpions."

"Maybe it'd be better to support him instead of trying to talk him out of it."

"You weren't here when he was tracking down Agent 17."

"No."

"He's a different person when he's doing things out of revenge," Jones said. "My worry is that if he tries to find this person, and it takes some time, he could lose himself."

"Maybe that was a worry before, but I don't think it would be now. Mia wouldn't let him stray too far."

"Perhaps that's true."

"One thing's for sure, you're not gonna talk him out of doing this," Haley said. "His mind's made up. He's gonna do it. With or without us."

Jones sighed. "I know. Believe me, I know."

24

The next morning, Recker returned to the office, wanting to put his beef with Jones behind him. He still was planning on going after the person that shot Mia, and he was going to do it whether Jones approved of it or not, but today was about getting back into the hospital to see Mia. They went through the entire morning, continually checking the police updates, but they still were not allowing anyone in at that point. Recker started pacing around the office.

"How long are they gonna stay there?" Recker asked. "How long does it take to clean up a crime scene?"

"I'm sure they just want to make sure it's safe for everyone to return," Jones said.

"Well hurry up and make it happen. There are people in there that would like visitors. They can't close the place up forever. People would like to see their loved ones who are in there. Get their head out of their ass and pick up the pace."

"I'm sure they're proceeding as quickly as possible."

"And before you say something, I'm not only talking about Mia. I'm talking about all the patients that are in there. Some of them I'm sure are dealing with difficult problems and could face them better if they had family support."

"As I said, I'm sure the police realize that as well and are moving quickly. It's not like they shut the whole place down. Patients are still being cared for."

"Yeah, well, if they don't hurry it up, I'm going in there regardless if the cops are there or not."

"I would strongly advise against that," Jones said. "There is no reason to lose our heads and do something we would regret."

"I wouldn't regret it."

Jones knew that was as correct a statement as was ever made. "That I would regret."

"Where's Chris at, by the way?"

"You've been here for several hours. Are you telling me you just realized he wasn't here?"

"Well he was here when I got here."

"And he left over an hour ago," Jones said.

"Yeah, I saw him go."

"And you didn't question it?"

Recker shrugged. "I dunno. I just assumed he went out for lunch or something. I figured you would have said if there was an assignment."

"Even if there was an assignment, would you take it right now in your present state?"

"Depends on what it was. If it was something that could be cleaned up fairly quickly, probably. If it was something that might take days, probably not."

"Well, Chris went down to the hospital to see if he could get some information on when it might reopen."

"Oh. He checked in yet?"

"He has not."

Recker continued pacing around the office for another thirty minutes as Jones went back to work. Recker's thoughts were so focused on Mia that a tank could've come crashing through the building, and there was a decent chance that Recker wouldn't have noticed. That changed when Jones' phone started ringing. Recker instantly whipped his head around, wondering if it was Haley finally checking in. After all, Jones didn't have a lot of numbers plugged into his phone. Luckily, Recker wasn't left waiting. Jones' initial greeting told him exactly who it was.

"Chris, how are things going?"

"Good. I just got word that the hospital's going to open back up again around five o'clock today."

"Is that confirmed?"

"It's not official, no. I was down here hitting up some of the hospital staff and a couple police officers."

"Who did you tell them you were?" Jones asked.

"I just told them that my mother was a patient, and that I wanted to see her soon. So, I asked a police officer, and he said it'd probably be around five o'clock. Then I asked two separate hospital staff people who came out in front of the building for different things, and they both said the same thing. So, right now, it looks like five o'clock is the time."

"OK. Thanks, Chris. Good work."

"I'm gonna still hang around here a while to see if anything changes."

"All right, sounds good."

Jones put his phone back down on the table and looked at Recker, who was staring at him with bated breath.

"Well?" Recker said.

"The latest information Chris has got says the hospital is going to reopen for business at five o'clock today."

"He's sure?"

"That's the information he's gotten from the people he's talked to. He talked to a police officer and several hospital workers who confirmed it. Now, I suppose that could change, but at this point, that's apparently what they're leaning towards."

"What about police presence? Are they gonna stay there?"

"He didn't say. He's going to stay there for a while and see if he can pick up anything else. I guess we shall see."

Recker looked at the time. Still had more than a few hours to wait. There was going to be a lot of pacing for him to do.

"Am I going to have to call in carpet installers after you're done?" Jones asked. "You're going to wear out a hole in the floor."

"That's why you should have put in hardwood."

"I never thought you were going to turn out to be a master pacer. You've probably walked a marathon in here just today."

"You should try it sometime."

"I don't think I could afford it."

"How's that?"

"I think I would need to buy new legs after I was done."

Recker finally let out a smirk, though it was only fleeting. He continued pacing, occasionally stopping to look out the window, or go to the bathroom, or grab a drink from the refrigerator. He looked at the time what seemed like every two minutes.

"Why don't you sit down for a few minutes?" Jones asked.

"Can't."

"By the time you see Mia you'll be exhausted and will fall asleep before you get there."

"Not likely."

Recker continued wearing out the carpet for the next few hours, not able to sit down as he anticipated seeing Mia again. Once four o'clock came, he was as antsy as ever.

"I might just go down there now," Recker said. "That way I can go in right at five o'clock."

"They might not even open right at five," Jones replied. "Might be five-fifteen or five-thirty, something like that. Just relax. Once Chris gets a definite word, he'll let us know."

"I don't like just sitting here."

"You haven't sat since you've been here."

"You know what I mean."

"Maybe you should take an anxiety pill or something. I don't think I've ever seen you this worked up before."

"Mia's in the hospital, how am I supposed to be calm?"

"It's not like she's hanging on or something, she's going to be fine."

"How do you know? What if something happened? A complication, something went wrong, could be anything?"

"I think we would have heard."

"How?" Recker asked. "It's not like they have our phone numbers to call."

"Michael, you've got to calm yourself down. You're going to explode."

A few seconds later, Jones' phone rang again. Recker quickly went over to the desk, assuming it was Haley calling. He was right. It was.

"Chris, anything new?" Jones asked.

"No, nothing new. But I just wanted to let you know that the hospital is opening up again to visitors at five o'clock."

"Are you sure?"

"Absolutely. Some of the police have already started moving out. They're keeping a few on the first-floor level, just to keep a presence and to look out for any trouble. I've also heard they're going to have a couple roaming around the other floors just in case."

"Are they going to be screening people on the way in or anything?"

"Not from what I hear," Haley replied. "They're just gonna keep an eye out in case they see something funny. With Billings dead, they're not expecting any more trouble here, but, they just wanna be on the safe side."

"All right, thank you."

"I'm still gonna stay here for a little bit, see if anything changes."

"OK."

Recker looked like he could barely contain himself as he waited for Jones to tell him what that was all about.

"Well?"

"Looks as though five o'clock is now a definite," Jones answered.

Recker pounded his fist on the desk in excitement. "I'm gonna head down there now."

"What are you going to do for half an hour before it opens?"

Recker shrugged. "Wear out the sidewalk."

"I shouldn't have asked."

Before leaving, Recker printed out the pictures of every known Scorpion they had on file. Jones didn't say anything, but he knew why his partner was doing it. He was going to have Mia identify the person that shot her, so Recker would know what back to put the target on. Once all the pictures were printed out, Recker grabbed them and put them in his pocket, then raced for the door.

"Give Mia my love," Jones said.

"I will."

Once Recker got to the hospital, he met up with Haley

just outside the front. With most of the police leaving, Recker didn't think he had to hide himself now. He still had a baseball hat pulled down low and sunglasses on. He figured that was enough. He didn't need to bother with other disguises and such. Besides, he didn't want Mia to see him all tricked out like that. He still carried the disguise box in his car, just in case the situation on the way in looked like it might call for it, he could go back to the car quickly and do his thing. But judging from the growing crowd in front of the building, it looked like a few hundred more people were champing at the bit to get inside.

"How's everything going?" Recker asked.

"Good. Looks like there's gonna be an avalanche of people going in once they open up."

"Yeah. Can't blame them. They wanna see their loved ones."

"You look nervous," Haley said, observing his friend shift around in his stance. "You been pacing around this whole time at the office?"

"Shows, huh?"

Haley smiled. "Just a little."

"Wish they'd just do it now."

"Well, guess they gotta get everything in order first."

"Yeah, I suppose so."

"Hey, maybe when you're done, I can go up and see her too?"

"Why don't you just go in with me?" Recker asked.

"Nah, that's your time. You guys should get to be alone for a few minutes, have some privacy. I was just thinking maybe when you're finished. If you think she'd want me there."

"You know she would. She'd love to have you there."

"Good."

"Why don't you give me a half hour or so, then you come up."

"Is that enough time for you?"

"Yeah, it'll be fine."

"OK. I'll come up at five-thirty."

They waited patiently, or not so patiently in Recker's case, for another twenty-five minutes. The doors on the ground level of the hospital started opening up five minutes early.

"Looks like we're moving early," Recker excitedly said. "Almost feels like I'm meeting her for the first time again."

Haley smiled, thinking it was cute how he was acting. He could only hope he found someone to love like that at some point.

"Five-thirty?" Haley asked, double checking.

Recker tapped him on the shoulder. "I'll see you up there."

25

Recker stood just outside Mia's room, taking a deep breath before going in. He walked right up to the room without a problem. Though he was a little nervous about slipping past the police on the main floor, it turned out to be no issue at all. There were a few officers by the main doors, but they were just there observing everyone, making sure there were no problems. They didn't actually interact or stop anyone.

Recker pushed the door open, peeking inside. He saw Mia lying there on the bed, awake. Her eyes instantly went to the door once she saw it open. A huge smile came over her face when she saw who was standing there. Recker pushed the door open all the way and stepped inside, seeing Mia put her arms out to welcome him. Recker walked over to the bed and hugged her.

"How are you feeling?" Recker asked.

"Surprisingly not too bad. Your body just feels a little different after going through something like that."

"I know the feeling."

Mia smiled. "Yeah. I guess you do."

"You're OK though?"

"Yeah. I wouldn't say I feel good, but it's not bad either. I'm not really in pain. I guess the pain medication is working pretty well."

Recker leaned over and kissed her. "I'm sorry."

"Don't even go there. This is not on you. It's not your fault. It's just something that happened. It could've been anyone. In some weird way, I'm almost glad it was me."

"What?"

"Because it happened to me, it got you here. I already heard about what happened. The masked men that came in here and drove those men out."

"Oh."

"So, if it had happened to someone else, you might not have come. Maybe more people would have gotten hurt, maybe it would have taken longer, maybe a lot more bad things would have happened."

"You really have a certain way of looking at things," Recker said. "I was afraid I was going to lose you."

"I guess now you know what it's been like for me worrying about you."

Recker stared at her for a few seconds, thinking of how right she was. "Yeah. I guess I do."

"So, what exactly happened anyway?"

"You want the long or the short version?"

"Whichever one you want to tell."

"I'll go with the short," Recker said. "Basically, me, Chris, and Malloy came into the building through the parking garage and started taking out everyone we came across. Eventually we made it up to the fifth floor where you were, found you, got you into surgery."

"Malloy?"

"Police had the building surrounded. Called Vincent for help. Him and Malloy didn't hesitate."

"Wow. I guess sometimes it does pay to have friends in low places."

Recker laughed. "Yeah, sometimes it does."

"So how did you get in?"

"A few cops on Vincent's payroll let us slip by."

"Nobody else got hurt?" Mia asked.

"Malloy took one in the leg, but he'll be OK. I think one other person, I can't remember if it was a visitor or someone that worked here, but whoever it was, they'll be OK too."

"Well that's good."

"What was it all about?"

"A group called the Scorpions came in here because one of their leaders had been shot and was now in police custody. They didn't want him going to jail I guess."

"So, they did all that just to help someone escape?"

"As far as we can tell."

"Sounds like going to extremes."

"Some people think they can do whatever they want. That they can't be stopped."

"Is it over?"

"Should be here anyway," Recker answered. "The guy

they came in here for is now dead, so they won't be back here. There's no reason for it. Anyway, enough about that. Did they say when you're gonna be able to leave yet?"

"Uh, no, I don't think they've said yet. I think they just wanna give me another day to make sure everything's OK. They said I lost a good amount of blood, so..."

"Hopefully, it'll only be a few days, maybe a week at most."

"Yeah. I just don't wanna lie here for a week. It's so boring."

Recker laughed. "Says the woman who works at a hospital."

"It's a little different when you're the one lying in a bed all the time. It's better on the other end of it."

"Yeah, I guess it is at that."

As they talked, Recker had forgotten all about the pictures in his pocket. At that moment, nothing else seemed to matter. The only thing that mattered was her. And she seemed to be doing as well as could be under the circumstances. As they talked, and smiled, and laughed, the time flew by. Before they even knew it, there was a knock on the door. They looked over and saw Haley poking his head in.

"Hey!" Mia said, smiling widely.

"Mind if I come in?" Haley asked.

Recker looked at the time. "Wow. The time went fast."

"If you guys need more time, I can come back later."

"No, come on in," Mia said. "The more people here the better. It's been so boring here by myself."

Haley walked into the room, holding something

behind his back. Recker leaned over, trying to see what it was. After a few seconds, Haley brought his arm around to the front, revealing a bouquet of different colored flowers.

"These are for you," Haley said, walking over to the bed and kissing Mia on the cheek.

"Awe, they're beautiful, thank you."

"Picked them up at the flower shop downstairs."

"That's so thoughtful."

Haley then put them in a cup of water that was on the table next to her bed. He looked down at Recker, who was just staring up at him.

"You trying to upstage me?" Recker asked.

"Huh?"

"I come in here with nothing and you come in with flowers. You trying to steal her away from me or something?"

The three of them had a good laugh, though Mia quickly stopped as it hurt. "I'm just glad you both could be here. I wasn't sure when or if you would be coming."

"There's nothing that would've kept me away," Recker said.

"I can vouch for that," Haley replied.

A few minutes later, a doctor came in the room to check on his patient. "Ah, visitors."

"This is my boyfriend, Mike," Mia said. "And our friend, Chris."

Recker stood up and shook the doctor's hand. Haley did the same. Recker immediately started peppering the doctor with questions.

"How much longer is she gonna have to be here?"

"Uh, I would say a few more days," the doctor answered. "She lost quite a bit of blood, which has made her a little weak and lethargic. That's really the main issue right now. Other than that, she's looking fine. I just wanna keep her a few more days for observation, make sure she gets her strength back up."

Recker nodded, not having a problem with it. He just wanted whatever was best for her. "OK."

"Even after she's released though, I want her to take it easy at home. No lifting, moving things, things like that. Just relax, lie down, nothing strenuous."

"That's no problem."

The doctor then did a quick examination of Mia, then left the room. Recker wanted to show her the pictures but didn't want to make it seem like he was putting anything else before her.

"How long are you staying?" Mia asked.

"How long do you want me to stay?" Recker replied.

Mia smiled. "All night if you can."

"I'll stay until you fall asleep. Then I have something to do. But I'll be right back after that."

Recker took a gulp, then reached into his pocket and removed the pictures. He put them on Mia's lap.

"Do you think you can identify the man who did this to you?"

Mia picked up the photos and started looking through them. "There's a lot here."

"Just take your time. Be sure."

Mia looked through about thirty pictures before she got to the one that did it. She stared at it, her mind going back to that moment when he pointed the gun at her and pulled the trigger.

"You see him?" Recker asked, noticing her hesitation.

"This is the guy."

"You're sure?"

"I could never forget his face," Mia said, handing the picture back to Recker.

Recker took the picture and looked at it. "Bill Cummins."

"Promise me you're not gonna kill him?"

"What?"

"Mike, I don't want you to kill him out of revenge for me."

Recker sighed, not wanting to get in an argument over it while she was in the hospital. "Mia, if this guy was willing to kill you just for the sake of it, that means he's willing to do it to anybody else who gets in his way. He's a dangerous guy who needs to be taken off the street."

"So, let the police do it."

"I really don't wanna talk about this here. You just need to focus on getting better."

"Mike, I know how you are. You're gonna obsess over this thing until you find him. You morph into someone else. I don't want you to do that."

Recker could see she was starting to get heated and didn't want that to happen. He put his hands on her to try to calm her down.

"OK, OK. Just relax."

Recker handed the picture of Cummins to Haley, while he put the rest of them back in his pocket. Haley instinctively knew what that meant. Recker wanted him to start working on finding Cummins, while he stayed there with Mia, not wanting to upset her anymore.

"OK, well, I'm gonna head out now," Haley said. "Get back to work."

"Thanks for coming," Mia said.

Haley gave her another hug and kiss before leaving. "I'll, uh, check back in later."

Recker nodded at him.

"Please promise me you won't kill him because of me," Mia said.

"We shouldn't talk about this now."

"Promise me."

Recker sighed. "I promise I won't kill him just because of you."

Mia was tired, probably too tired to realize he could've contorted what he said to mean just about anything to suit his purposes. Recker continued sitting there for a little while, talking with Mia, until she drifted off to sleep about half an hour later. He thought about leaving, but ultimately decided against it. He wanted his face to be what she saw when she eventually awoke. Cummins would have to wait. If only for a little bit.

26

Five days had passed, and Mia had been released from the hospital. Jones told Recker to take a week off to help take care of her, which he did. As much as he wanted to go after Cummins, he just couldn't put that ahead of Mia's well-being. Not after everything she'd done for him over the years. He had to be there for her, no matter what.

But that didn't mean the search for Cummins wasn't moving full steam ahead. Even though it was against his better judgment, Jones continued looking for him, figuring it was better that he did it, instead of Recker going full-out crazy, looking for the man. At least if Jones did it, it would be in more of an orderly fashion. Haley helped in the search as well, but with Recker on the sidelines for the time being, he was the one managing the rest of the workload. If something heavy came up, they agreed they could call Recker in, but luckily, there was nothing that required the both of them. Just some minor issues that Haley could take care of by himself.

Mia was lying on the couch, watching TV, when Recker came in from the kitchen, bringing her a bowl of tomato soup, one of her favorites. She smiled at him as she took the bowl.

"This must be driving you crazy, huh?"

Recker shook his head. "Not as much as you'd think."

"Oh, so you're starting to get used to being Mr. Mom?"

Recker laughed. "I hardly think making you something to eat qualifies as Mr. Mom. It's not like we got a bunch of kids running around or anything."

Mia suddenly lost the smile on her face as she thought about what he said. Recker realized it was probably the wrong thing to say, considering the baby they once lost.

"Hey, the doctor said it won't impact your ability to have kids."

"I know," Mia said. "It still makes me wonder and worry though. What if it does?"

"It's not something you need to worry about now. Right now, you just need to worry about getting your strength back and getting back to normal. Everything else is a discussion for another time."

Mia smiled at him. "You're right."

Mia took a few sips of her soup as Recker went back into the kitchen and cleaned up. A minute later there was a knock on the door. Recker hurried out of the kitchen, looking a little flustered. He wasn't expecting anybody. Jones and Haley always let him first know if they were coming over. Recker went over to the closet and grabbed his gun off the top shelf. He went over to the door and looked out the peephole. He took a step back and looked at Mia, a sense of relief on his face, as he put his gun in the back of his pants. Recker opened the door, letting Tyrell in.

"What are you doing here?" Recker asked.

Tyrell tapped him on the chest as he waltzed in. "Hey, nice to see you too."

Recker closed the door. "A phone call to let us know you were coming would've been nice."

"Yeah, but I wanted to make it a surprise." Tyrell then looked at Mia. "There's my sister!"

Mia smiled, happy to see him. "Hey Ty!"

"Sorry I couldn't make it to the hospital. Had a lot of family stuff going on."

"That's OK."

Tyrell went over to Mia and gave her a hug, then sat down next to her. "How you feeling?"

"Pretty good considering."

Recker came over and sat down on a chair across from them.

"Hey, you know what I just realized?" Tyrell asked.

"What's that?" Recker said.

"We've all been shot!" Tyrell then laughed. "Isn't that something? A little something for us all to bond over."

Recker raised an eyebrow. "Guess some people bond over less."

"You don't mind me just dropping in like this, do you?"

"Well..."

"Of course not," Mia said. "You know we love it when you drop by."

Recker smiled, though it didn't look genuine. "Yes. We sure do."

The three of them sat there talking for about twenty minutes before Recker's phone started ringing. He walked into the kitchen and picked up his phone, which he left on the table.

"Yeah?"

"How is Mia?" Jones asked.

"She's doing good. Tyrell just stopped over."

"That's good. Almost perfect timing."

"Why?"

Jones almost hated to say, knowing what would happen next. "Because you're probably going to leave. It would be nice knowing someone was still there with her."

"Where would I go?"

"We found Cummins."

"Where?"

Jones cleared his throat. "He's at the same apartment that Billings was at when Chris had his run-in with him."

"How long's he been there?"

"Just arrived."

"How do you know?"

"Well, it's a culmination of some of the things we've been doing while you've been home. Basically, we thought he might be there, so Chris went there to check it out. And Cummins just showed up."

"I'm on the way."

"Do you want me to just have Chris handle it?"

"No, I'm coming," Recker said. "Tell him to wait for me."

"What if Cummins leaves before you get there?"

"I'm coming."

"Understood."

Recker hung up, then walked back in the living room. Mia could tell by the look on his face, that he had something to say that he was apprehensive about.

"Umm, Chris needs help with something. I really should go."

"I understand," Mia said.

Recker then looked at Tyrell. "You mind hanging here for a while with her?"

"Hey, me sitting here with a beautiful woman while you're not around, you sure you trust me with that?"

Recker smiled, then removed his gun, just letting it dangle next to his leg. "Remember, I know where you live."

Tyrell laughed. "Point taken, point taken."

"I'll be back as soon as I can."

Recker went over to Mia and gave her a kiss before leaving. As he was on the road, he called Haley to let him know he was on the way. Haley reinforced that he would just sit on everything until his partner got there. By the time Recker arrived, about half an hour had passed. Luckily for him, Cummins hadn't left the apartment building. As soon as Recker got there, he found Haley, and went over to his car, hopping in the passenger seat.

"Hey, how's Mia?" Haley asked.

"She's good. Tyrell's sitting with her until I get back."

"Oh. Good."

"How many we looking at?" Recker asked.

"Three. Cummins and two of his cronies."

"What are they doing here?"

"Beats me. Must be some things they're trying to clear out of Billings' place. Information or papers or something."

"Something they don't want to fall into the hands of someone else," Recker said.

"Yeah, probably. So how you wanna do this? Wait until they come out or head in after them?"

"Waiting doesn't appeal to me much."

"Didn't think it would."

"If we wait until they come outside and we follow them, they could go just about anywhere."

"Could lead us to the others too," Haley said.

"Or lead us into a more dangerous spot. And it'd be out in the open and in public, which I don't like."

"We're going in?"

Recker looked at him and smiled. "We're going in."

"Let me go in first."

"Why?"

"They saw your face at the hospital," Haley answered. "If they got someone looking out, they'll know trouble's coming. If they see me though, I'm just a regular guy they don't know."

Recker nodded, knowing it was a good point. "You're right."

"Once I'm in, I'll let you know."

Haley got out of the car and headed toward the apartment building. He just hoped it wasn't a repeat of the last time he was there, surprising him by walking out. Luckily, it wasn't. He went into the building and headed up the steps until he got to Billings' floor. He let his partner know they were good to go.

"I'm in the stairwell. I've got a straight view to the apartment."

"On my way," Recker said.

Once Recker was out of the car, he sprinted to the building, quickly getting inside. He made his way up the steps to get to Haley's position.

"See anything?" Recker asked.

"Not yet. I assume they're still in there, but I can't say for sure."

Recker took a quick look around. "Well, we'll have to make this quick. We can't stay here for long in case someone else comes along."

Recker and Haley emerged from the stairwell, heading straight for Billings' apartment. The door was closed, but once they stood just outside of it, they could hear people talking inside. It sounded like they were getting pretty animated. Recker made a few motions to Haley, wondering if they should knock or just bust their way through the door. Haley shrugged, not having a strong feeling about it either way. After a few seconds, Recker decided it was better to not announce their presence. Him and Haley both took a few steps back, then together, almost put their collective feet through the door. Pieces of the frame of the door splintered off as it broke off.

The men inside were shocked and surprised by the

intrusion. They immediately went for their guns, but Recker and Haley were coming in shooting. They both shot at the first man they saw. There were actually four Scorpions inside the room, as one of them was already there, waiting for the others. Two of them went down instantly at the hands of Recker and Haley. By the time the other two removed their guns, Recker and Haley had turned their attention to them. Cummins was able to get a shot off, though it missed wildly, going well over Recker's shoulder and into the wall. Recker's shot did not miss though. Cummins hit the floor almost immediately after the bullet entered his chest from Recker's gun. Haley had already taken care of the remaining member of the group.

Recker could see that Cummins was still breathing, so he walked over to him, standing over him. As Cummins looked at the man who had just shot him, he remembered his face from the hospital. Cummins reached for his gun, which had flown out of his hand upon being shot, but it was too far away, and it hurt too much to move. He was dying and would probably be dead within minutes.

"I remember you," Cummins said hoarsely.

"Good. I was hoping you would."

Cummins spit out some blood. "What for? What'd I do to you?"

"That woman you shot in the hospital was my girlfriend."

Cummins spit out some more blood as he laughed, not believing the unbelievable bad luck he had from that one incident. "That's what this was about. All of it? The hospital? This? A woman?"

Recker nodded. "That's it."

"Of all the dumb luck. Who are you anyway?"

"I'm The Silencer."

Cummins eyes widened, hardly believing it. "Wow. We really screwed this up, huh?"

"I would say so."

"Mike, we gotta go," Haley said, worried about witnesses and the police, who were sure to be coming.

Recker nodded, knowing there was no time to stay. But he wasn't going to leave Cummins alive. Not even for an extra thirty seconds. He didn't deserve a second of extra life. Recker pointed his gun back at Cummins, who already knew he was dying, and pulled the trigger. Cummins' eyes instantly closed. Recker stood over him for a second, but Haley rushed over to the door, grabbing Recker by the arm to pull him along. The two rushed back down the hallway and sprinted down the stairs as they exited the building. Once they got back in their cars, they went across the street, waiting for the police to arrive. The cops showed up about five minutes later, Recker and Haley still watching.

"Well, at least that's over," Haley said.

"It's not over," Recker replied. "There's still a lot more Scorpions out there. And it's gonna be my personal mission to get them out of this city. It's not over. This is just the beginning."

ZEROED IN PREVIEW

Thank you for reading Lethal Force. Please enjoy the following three chapter preview of the next book in The Silencer Series, Zeroed In.

27

A month had passed since the takeover of the hospital by The Scorpions. Things around the city had been pretty quiet since then, at least as far as that group was concerned. Recker and Haley were still pretty busy doing their usual thing, though everything was pretty easy according to their standards. The Scorpions had gone into hiding, having to regroup after losing a couple of their top guys. Though the hope throughout the city was that they had left, licking their wounds after realizing they couldn't run over everyone in their way, Recker and the gang knew better. It was only a matter of time before they reappeared again. And they would likely be just as lethal and violent as before. Maybe even more so, thinking that they needed to be even tougher and badder than ever to survive.

Recker had just gotten to the office, taking most of the morning off. It was Mia's return to work, and he wanted to make sure she was up for it before she left. She was actually ready to go back a week before that, but Recker was successful in convincing her to take the extra time. He had more fears about her going back than she did. He was worried about something bad happening again, even though he knew what happened the previous month was a once in a lifetime type of event. Mia wasn't that worried herself. She knew what happened would probably never happen again. She didn't have any fears about going back. But the worry was still evident across Recker's face as he walked by his friends.

"Everything will be fine," Jones said.

"What?"

"Mia will be fine."

"Who said she wouldn't?"

"Your face says so. I can see it written across it."

"I'm not worried," Recker said.

"Uh, huh. So that's why you took the morning off? So that's why you have that look on your face? Because you're not worried?"

"I took the morning off because it was her first day back at work. It had nothing to do with me being worried."

"Oh, OK."

"Instead of analyzing me, how about we talk about what's going on?"

Jones looked perplexed. He wasn't aware of anything happening at the moment. "Going on? What's going on?"

"I dunno. I assume something is. Isn't there usually something?"

"Usually so. But not at the moment."

"Oh." Recker looked around the office, noticing the absence of one of his partners. "So where's Chris?"

"Out."

"Doing what?"

"He had an assignment."

"You just told me nothing was happening."

"I said there's nothing happening at the moment. And there is not."

"But you just said Chris was on an assignment."

"He was. He's not now."

"You just said..."

"I said he *was* on an assignment. That job has been completed. He's on his way back to the office now. So therefore, since we have no other jobs to do at the present time, nothing is happening, and nothing is going on. See how that works?"

"Oh, you're being a wiseguy now?"

"Well I have to take something from you, don't I?"

"You just type away there. Leave the humor to me."

"So how is Mia, anyway? Ready to go back to work?"

"She was ready to go back two weeks ago."

"She's a tough woman."

"She is. Hopefully she never goes through a situation like that again."

"Mike, the odds of a situation like that happened again to her are probably astronomical."

"I know. It's just... if it happens once, it can happen again."

"The only way I could see it happening again is if The

Scorpions realize she's your girlfriend and deliberately try something because of that."

"I know. And that's what worries me."

"But they won't find that out."

"But what if they do?" Recker asked.

"How would they?"

Recker shrugged. "I don't know. How does anyone find anything out? Dig a little, loose lips, in the right spot at the right time, or the wrong spot for that matter. Just by mistake. Things like that happen."

"I don't think you have to worry about that."

"We'll see. How long until Chris gets back?"

Jones looked at the time. "Probably twenty minutes or so."

"What was he working on?"

"Domestic violence situation. A man texted his wife that he was going to kill her. They had been separated for the past month."

"He have any problems with it?"

"No. He had a little chat with the man and took care of it without a problem."

Another ten minutes went by, with Recker checking out his gun cabinet to pass the time, making sure everything was cleaned and ready to go. His phone started ringing, and he instinctively thought it might have been Mia, having a problem about returning to work. He was surprised to see that it wasn't, and maybe a little happy too. Though upon seeing that it was Malloy, he knew something was probably up, and not for the better.

"Hey, what's up?"

"You know, the usual," Malloy replied.

"Something bad?"

"That's the usual, isn't it?"

"I suppose it is. So what's up now?"

"Vincent would like to chat with you."

"What for?"

"I dunno. Something about The Scorpions I think."

"They back?"

"Did they leave?"

"What else is up?"

"I don't know. I'm pretty sure it's just about The Scorpions. What exactly, or anything else, I'm not sure."

"What's going on with them?"

"I dunno. Boss just said he wanted to meet with you."

"When?"

"As soon as you can make it. Now would be ideal he said. But tomorrow would work too if you can't make it today."

"Uh, no, I can make it now. Where? Usual spot I take it?"

"You got it. It's lunchtime."

Recker laughed. "So it is."

"So I'll tell him you'll be there?"

"I'll be there."

"See you then."

After Recker hung up the phone, he stood next to his cabinet, just staring at the wall. His actions weren't lost on Jones, who could tell something was on his mind. There always was something when he did that.

"What was that about?" Jones asked.

"Vincent wants a meet."

"What for?"

"Something about The Scorpions."

"What about them?"

"I don't know. That's what he wants to talk about, apparently."

"And I take it you're going?"

"Don't I always?"

Jones let out a sigh. "Unfortunately yes. You always do."

"Doesn't it usually wind up being good that I do?"

"That's debatable."

"For who?"

"For us."

"Usually always get something out of it," Recker said.

"Yes, more headaches and more problems. If that is what you are referring to, then yes, we most certainly get something out of it."

"I was talking about information."

"I guess sometimes we get that too."

"David, Vincent doesn't just call for a meeting to shoot the breeze. If he says it's something about The Scorpions, I gotta imagine it's pretty good and is worth our while."

"Perhaps."

"All I've got to lose is my time."

"Well, I wouldn't say that's all you've got to lose, but, I know you're going, so there's that."

"You make it sound like you're not interested in their whereabouts?"

"To be honest, I'd be quite happy if they moved on and we never heard about them again."

"We both know what the odds of that are," Recker said. "They're not going away. They're just regrouping. And when they reappear again... watch out. I have a feeling they're going to be worse than ever."

"Well there's something to look forward to. I was hoping that they would decide the effort to remain here is too great and they would move on for easier pastures somewhere else."

Recker shook his head. "Their pride is hurt now. Wounded. They won't, can't, admit defeat that easily. They can't let it get out that they were run out of somewhere. Hurts their ego. And it makes it easier for others to stand up to them, thinking they're not as big and tough and bad as they've heard about. No, they can't leave. Not now."

Jones sighed. "So once again we are going to get side-tracked from our main objective to deal with some riff-raff that's going to take up most of our time."

"We both know that's the way it goes sometimes."

"Unfortunately yes. And it happens too often."

"All comes with the territory."

"Are you going to wait until Chris comes back?"

"No, I'll just head out now," Recker answered. "I don't need backup for Vincent. Just keep him on standby in case something develops while I'm gone."

"So I'll put him on speed dial is what you're saying."

Recker smirked. "Funny."

"And you say I never take any of your traits."

"What'd I tell you before? Leave the humor to me."

Recker closed his gun cabinet, then got ready to leave. "Want me to call you on the way back?"

"Only if you have something interesting to tell me."

"Don't I always?"

"What did I tell you before? Unfortunately, yes."

"Funny man."

"I'm trying to spread my wings," Jones said.

"Well, don't spread them too far. Stick to what suits you best."

"So being a thorn in your side?"

Recker smiled as he walked out the door. "See you later, Professor."

28

After entering the building, Recker exchanged handshakes with Malloy. Recker looked him over, noticing that he didn't look the worse for wear.

"Doesn't even getting shot get you a vacation?"

Malloy smiled. "Who needs them? Aren't we already living in Paradise?"

"If this is Paradise, I'd hate to see your definition of Hell."

Malloy snickered. "Might be the same thing."

Recker nodded. "Might be at that."

Recker then walked down to the end of the restaurant, finding Vincent at his usual and favorite table. He had just ordered and given the menu back to the waitress as Recker sat down across from him.

"Not too late to get you something," Vincent said.

"I'm good, thanks."

Vincent smiled. "I always forget, you get that good

home cooking."

"Not too much lately."

Vincent nodded. "How is she doing these days?"

"As good as can be expected. Going back to work."

"Good to hear. I'm glad for the both of you. She's a tough one."

"She is."

"I wouldn't expect anything less from a girlfriend of yours."

"Well, I can't really take any credit for that," Recker said. "That's all her."

Vincent coughed, then cleared his throat. "Getting pleasantries out of the way, I'm sure you've got other things to do, so I'll get straight to the point on this one. I'm sure you're curious what this is about."

"Crossed my mind."

"The Scorpions. I'm hearing they have regrouped."

"Figured they would. I didn't expect them to take that beating and lick their tails and run. I assumed they'd be back."

"And they are. Now."

"I haven't heard anything."

"I have," Vincent said. "They've got new leadership in place and it looks like they're ready to do some things."

"What kind of things?"

"First is, they're looking to put down some roots. They're staying for a while."

"Well, I guess I'll have a little something to say about that."

"They're planning to have something to say about that too."

"What do you mean?"

"They know it was you behind that whole hospital thing."

"How?"

"Who else would it be?"

"Couldn't take one for the team and say it was you?" Recker said with a laugh.

"Doesn't suit my purposes at the moment."

Recker shrugged, not really concerned if they knew it was him or not. "Doesn't really matter."

"Maybe not yet. But let me tell you, my friend, they are gunning for you. You, right now, are their number one target. Their number one enemy. You. And you alone. And they are planning on zeroing in."

"That makes two of us. They're my number one target too. And I'm gonna zero in on them. And I am not gonna rest until the rest of them are put in the ground with their friends."

"I knew that would be your intention. I just wanted to warn you that they're planning on doing everything within their means to find you."

"Let them. I'm not afraid of them. How do you fit into this?"

"I don't. Not yet, at least. They're still planning on side-stepping me as much as possible for the moment. I don't see that changing until they get you out of the picture."

Recker smiled. "You mean if, don't you?"

"Of course. I've learned to never bet against you over the years, no matter what the odds."

"What about the leadership group? You know who it is?"

"Kind of similar to before. I believe they're using a three-headed monster so to speak. A three-man leadership group to make decisions for the bunch."

"Got names?"

Vincent reached into his pocket and removed a slip of paper, then slid it across the table. Recker picked it up and saw three names on it.

"Mind reading now?"

Vincent grinned. "I think I know you well enough by now to anticipate some of your questions."

"Know anything about these guys?"

"I've done some background on them, as I'm sure you will as well. Nothing that particularly stands out other than they're long-term members of the group. I think all exceeding ten years."

"So no new ideas or fresh concepts, probably. They'll stick to what they know best."

"Most likely."

"They can target me all they want, they're not gonna find me, so that's of no consequence to me."

"All it takes is one slip-up."

Recker shook his head. "Won't happen. Besides me, any ideas on what they got tabs on?"

"That I do not. With a group like that it could be almost anything."

"How do you know they're still planning on staying out of your way?"

"I had a meeting with these men yesterday," Vincent answered. "They assured me of such."

They talked for another twenty minutes or so, almost all of it about The Scorpions. By the time Recker left, he didn't feel any differently than he had before, but at least he had the names of the leaders now. They already had their names and faces from the check they did before, but now they knew who was calling the shots. When Recker exited the diner, Malloy escorted him outside. Along with the usual guard at the door, the three men made some small talk before Recker had to go. Recker happened to look across the street and saw a light blue car parked along the street, with a couple of men inside. As soon as Recker made eye contact, the men looked away. Recker didn't stare long, but looked long enough to recognize the two faces as Scorpion members. He continued talking to the other two men, not wanting to make a big deal out of it.

"Just so you know, you might wanna tell Vincent to change his eating habits," Recker said.

"Why?" Malloy asked.

"Don't look, just trust what I say."

"OK?"

"There's two Scorpions sitting across the street looking at us."

Malloy and the guard continued talking to Recker like he had never informed them of the men, giving the Scorpions no indication that they had been discovered.

"You sure?" Malloy asked.

"Positive. Recognize them from the pictures we got laid out in the office. It's them."

"I guess the question is now... what are they doing here? They looking to get tabs on Vincent's whereabouts and movements? Or are they looking for you?"

"Could be both," Recker replied. "They might be trying to find me first, then after I'm gone, then come after him. I think right now I'm their first priority."

"Makes sense."

"Either way, they're gonna have to be dealt with."

"You know anything about this meeting they had with Vincent yesterday?"

Malloy shook his head. "No, I didn't hear the details."

"Strange. Don't you always?"

Malloy grinned. "Not this time."

"Well, whatever the case, if they take off after I leave, you can be sure they're after me at the moment. If not, then it's you."

"I'll walk you to your car."

Recker thought it was an odd statement, considering Malloy had never offered to do that before. He knew something was up. Malloy wanted to talk to Recker in private, without the other guard listening in. He didn't want anyone to know he was talking about Vincent's business without authorization. That was a no-no in Vincent's world. And Malloy was in such good standing, he wasn't going to do it in front of other employees. As they walked to Recker's car, Malloy finally opened up.

"About this meeting yesterday, I did hear a few things."

"So you were there?"

"Possibly. Didn't want to say with wandering ears around."

They stopped and faced each other once they got back to Recker's SUV. "What do you know?"

"I know they're planning on putting a terror-lockdown on this city in the coming weeks. Bank jobs, violent robberies, assaults, you name it, they're planning on doing it. They want to put a fear into this city over what went down at the hospital. They especially want to send a message to you that you haven't won. They're angry. They know you were the one behind that."

"I figured they would assume it."

"They don't know the real reason behind it. You know, Mia and all. They think it was just about them. As far as I know, they don't know the connection between you. I just thought I'd let you know so you weren't wondering."

"I appreciate that."

"The other thing is they assume you have two partners, based on the hospital thing."

"I do."

"Yeah, but not the two that they think. They assume it's like a three-man squad that goes out there. So it's just you and Chris, but they think it's three of you out there instead of two."

Recker glanced over at the car across the street, not turning his head directly at them so they didn't think he noticed them. They were still there.

"You know anything about what they're planning?" Recker asked. "Any specifics?"

"No, just in general terms. I know they're planning on sending you a message somehow. How they're doing that, I don't know. But they said it's gonna be big and loud, so whatever that means."

"Thanks for the tips."

"Figured you should know."

"Wonder why Vincent didn't say."

"You know how he is. He won't say anything unless he thinks it's necessary. He likes being the one with the most knowledge and holding it over your head."

"So why are you telling me?"

Malloy looked past Recker and focused on a couple of other cars as he formulated the answer in his mind. "I dunno. I guess because I think he's making a mistake with all this."

"How so?"

"He's letting The Scorpions play in his sandbox for a while instead of taking them out right away. You can't let guys like this get a foothold, because once they do, they'll want more, and more, and more. This thing they have with you is only a stepping stone for them. Once they feel you're out of the way, or they just go around you completely, it's only a matter of time before they go after him."

"So why's he hesitating on them so much?"

Malloy shook his head. "To be honest, I'm not sure. I thought it was just because he didn't want another war so close on the heels of Nowak, but I don't think that's it. We've got enough men to fight them."

"I thought so too."

"He hasn't said this, and I could be off base, but I think he's hoping that you take them out for him. If he lets you do it, he probably only has to give minimal support, he stays in the clear, he doesn't have to risk losing men, and you do all the heavy lifting for him."

"I kind of figured it was something like that."

"Like I said, though, that's just my gut feeling on it. He hasn't said that directly."

"It would make sense though."

"Yeah, well, if you need my help, you got it. Just ask."

"Vincent wouldn't like that."

Malloy sighed. "I know. But the person who's on top doesn't always see the big picture as clearly as the ones who are on the front line, do they?"

"I would agree with that."

"These guys are bad dudes and they need to be eliminated. I know a lot of people would think that's strange coming from someone like me."

"I don't."

"You're an exception. I've done a lot of bad things in my time, and some I should be locked up for, but I've never hurt someone who didn't deserve it or who didn't know what they were getting into. These guys hurt people just to hurt them. That's the difference."

Recker nodded, understanding what he was saying completely. "You hear anything about them recruiting?"

"Yeah, I think they got some feelers out there. Don't think it's in full swing yet though."

"Why not?"

"They need time to get people in and trust them.

They've never had to do something like this before. You put a hurting on them. They've always just brought one or two people in every few months or so, you know, as things came along. They never had to go out and actively solicit people. They just came to them naturally. This is new territory for them. They gotta take their time to get the right people so they know who they're getting."

"That makes it better for us," Recker said. "But it means we gotta hit them before they really do get more people in."

"I agree. Right now, there's what, fifty, sixty people? If we let them go for a while and they get in full recruiting mode, they could pick up another fifty, seventy-five guys. They gotta be taken out in full in the next couple of weeks."

"Take two or three out a day, piece of cake, right? Have it sewed up in three weeks."

Malloy smiled. "I was hoping for bigger chunks at a time. Why settle for smaller numbers?"

"So how you gonna swing working this without Vincent finding out?"

"I'll just tell him things come up that I gotta take care of. Won't be anything new or unusual. I'll just head out like I always do. Tell him the details later."

"Well when Scorpions start showing up dead the day after you're always ducking out, don't you think he's gonna put two and two together?"

"Not if I do it right."

"OK. I guess if something comes up that I need a hand with, I'll give you a call."

Malloy nodded. "And if I hear specifics on anything, I'll pass it along to you."

Recker then shook hands with him. "Sounds like a deal."

"What are you gonna do about them?" Malloy asked, barely giving a nod of his head, though it was clear he was referring to the Scorpions that were watching them.

"Oh. Guess I'm gonna have to duck them somewhere."

"Need a hand?"

"Why, got some free time?"

"Well, you wanna start taking them out? No time like the present. If they're after you, won't come back to Vincent at all. They'll assume it's your work."

"What'd you have in mind?"

"You keep driving to a specific place. I'll get a sniper in place. When they get there, we take them out."

Recker smiled. "You got a sniper on speed dial?"

"There's one here every time Vincent's here. Just in case."

Recker briefly looked at a few of the surrounding buildings, trying to figure out where the man would be located, though he couldn't initially see anything. It didn't surprise him though. A man like Vincent would always take the utmost precautions, especially after shots had been taken at him before.

"Vincent won't realize you're shifting your man around?"

Malloy shook his head. "Nah. I take care of all that. If you leave now, drive for about twenty minutes, stop, he'll take the shots, then be back before Vincent leaves."

"All neat and tidy."

"That's the idea. Vincent's usually got another hour here, so we gotta move quick if you wanna do it."

"Your man won't tell Vincent he was redirected?"

"He'll think the order came from him. It'll be fine, trust me. I know how to rework things. Don't worry about me."

"OK," Recker said, hopping into his car. "You're in the driver's seat."

29

As Recker pulled out of the parking lot, Malloy went back over to the front entrance of the diner. He stood there and made small talk with the guard, looking out of the corner of his eye at the car across the street. Once Recker got on the street and started driving away, the car with the Scorpions started up and drove after him. That was Malloy's cue. He got on his phone and called the sniper that was nearby.

"Hey, you see that blue car that just pulled out?" Malloy asked.

"Going the same direction as Recker?"

"That's it."

"Yeah."

"Two occupants. Front seat. Take them out."

"Where?"

"I'm gonna have Recker go to the warehouse down by the river. You know the one."

"When?"

"Get there now. The guys in the car are Scorpions."

"What about Recker?"

"He's fine. Pass."

"On my way."

"Let me know when it's done."

"Will do."

Recker drove for about ten minutes, not knowing exactly where he was going. He figured Malloy would call at some point. If he wanted to, he could have lost the Scorpions on his own. It wouldn't have been much of a challenge for him. But, Malloy was right. This way was better. They had to start eliminating Scorpions a little at a time, whenever they could find them. Once they started building their ranks again, the job would get infinitely tougher. As he was sitting at a light, with the car the Scorpions were in three cars behind him, Recker's phone finally rang.

"Down by the river," Malloy said. "Remember that little warehouse that we used to set Nowak up in?"

"I remember."

"Go in there and wait."

"Should I get out of my car?"

"Doesn't matter. My guy's on his way there. He'll be in place by the time you get there. That's why I waited to call you, so he could get there first."

"OK. I'm on my way there."

Recker made sure he didn't lose his tail, which was somewhat different for him. Usually, he was driving faster and with a lot more turns, weaving in and out of traffic.

This time, he drove at a nice and steady pace, making sure the people behind him kept up with him. A couple of times, his normal instincts took over, and he had to consciously slow down, reminding himself that he wasn't trying to lose anybody on this occasion.

Recker arrived at the abandoned trucking facility after another twenty minutes in the car. The gate was slightly open, so Recker got out of his car to open it further. He got back in his car and drove all the way in, stopping once he got to the office building. He kept the gate open so his followers could come in as well, though he didn't know the exact plan on taking them out. That was the only part that really bothered him. He didn't know exactly how Malloy planned on taking them out, other than a sniper was probably already in place somewhere. Recker didn't like being kept in the dark about anything, especially when his life was involved. He got back out of the car again and milled around the front door. He kept peeking at the gate, waiting to see if the blue car had arrived yet, though he didn't see it. The door to the office was unlocked, so Recker went in. It didn't look like anything had changed since the last time he was there. It was still dusty, dirty, and unused.

Recker looked out the window, though he still didn't see the car. It wasn't waiting by the gate and it hadn't pulled in. While he was waiting, he called Jones to let him know where he was, since he didn't go right back to the office after the meeting.

"How's things there?" Recker asked.

"Fine. Is your meeting over?"

"Yeah. I, uh, took a detour on the way back."

"I'm sure you will explain that further, right?"

"When I came out of the diner, I noticed two Scorpions sitting across the street in a car. I assume they were looking for me, waiting for me to come out so they could tail me."

"How would they know you were there?"

"I don't know."

"I mean, that's kind of random, don't you think?"

"Could be they are following Vincent, hoping he would eventually meet me," Recker replied. "Might've had people set up all around the city hoping I'd show up."

"Possibly."

"Apparently, according to Vincent, I'm there number one target right now."

"Well that's hardly surprising."

"No, it's not. Vincent said he just had a meeting with their new leadership group yesterday. He gave me their names."

"Good."

"He also said they're planning on some big stuff. They're gonna be more violent than ever."

"Again, not that surprising."

"They also are planning on sending me some kind of message, though I don't know what that might be."

"Hmm. Sounds rather ominous."

"Yeah, and a little scary too," Recker said. "I just hope their message to me doesn't cost innocent people their lives."

"So I take it this detour of yours is trying to lose them following you?"

"Well, in a way, yeah, kind of."

"Would you like to explain that better?"

"I'm losing them permanently."

"Oh," Jones replied, knowing exactly what that meant. "How are you doing that? Or shouldn't I ask?" Jones knew it was sometimes better for his mental state if he didn't know all the details.

"I'm sure it'll please you to know that I'm not lifting a finger."

Jones hesitated before answering, not having a clue as to what was going on. "Uh, you did say you were losing them permanently, did you not?"

"Malloy is helping to diffuse the situation. I led the car here to the river, you know, where we did that thing with Nowak. He's got a sniper here who's gonna take them out."

"So Vincent is helping?"

"No, not quite. Malloy's doing this off the books."

"Wait a minute. You're telling me Malloy is authorizing killing Scorpions without his boss' approval."

"That's right."

"Uh, wow. That's kind of a powder keg in the making, don't you think?"

"Maybe," Recker answered. "Malloy seems to think it's not a problem so long as it's kept hush-hush."

"I don't know about that."

"Well, it's not really our problem."

"Why is Malloy interjecting himself into this situation?"

"He doesn't share Vincent's strategy, which I kind of question myself. Maybe he's got something bigger in mind, but I don't know why Vincent's taking a back seat on this. Anyway, Malloy knows the longer the Scorpions are allowed to remain here, the more Vincent's going to eventually become their target. Malloy knows it's better to get rid of them now than allow them to stay here for six months and build their troops back up. Now's the time to strike and get them out."

"As much as it pains me to say it, I agree. With every battle or conflict in history, the best time to strike was when the enemy was already reeling, before they had a chance to regroup. In theory, that time is now."

As they were talking, two loud booms rang out in the clear blue sky. Recker instantly looked through the window, knowing what that meant. Jones heard the pops as well.

"Oops. Looks like I gotta go."

"Should I ask?" Jones said.

"No, you shouldn't. I'll see you later."

Recker sprinted out of the office and got back in his car. He raced to the front gate, then got out of his car and looked down the street. He instantly saw the blue car parked across the street, only fifteen or twenty feet down. Recker got back in his car and slowly drove past the Scorpions, looking inside their vehicle as he passed. He saw both men in the front seats slumped over. The driver's head was resting up against the steering wheel, while the passenger was tilted on his side, his arm slightly hanging out the window. Recker knew it was pointless to look around to see where the shots came from, though he had a good general direction. He then looked in his rearview mirror and saw a tan car peel onto the street and race in the opposite direction. He thought about calling Malloy to let him know it was done, but he figured the sniper would do that, anyway.

There was nothing left for him to do now. Nothing but wait. Wait for the message that he knew was coming. And after the Scorpions found out what just happened with the crew that was following him, Recker was sure that message would come through a little louder, and a little clearer. He just hoped it was only meant for him and nobody innocent got caught up in it. Now, it was just a matter of when that message would be received.

ABOUT THE AUTHOR

Mike Ryan is a USA Today Bestselling Author. He lives in Pennsylvania with his wife, and four children. He's the author of the bestselling Silencer Series, as well as many others. Visit his website at www.mikeryanbooks.com to find out more about his books, and sign up for his newsletter. You can also interact with Mike via Facebook, and Instagram.

facebook.com/mikeryanauthor
instagram.com/mikeryanauthor

ALSO BY MIKE RYAN

Continue reading The Silencer Series with the next book in the series, Zeroed In.

Other Books:

The Eliminator Series

The Extractor Series

The Cain Series

The Cari Porter Series

The Ghost Series

The Brandon Hall Series

A Dangerous Man

The Last Job

The Crew

CPSIA information can be obtained
at www.ICGtesting.com
Printed in the USA
LVHW082056110821
695090LV00014B/156/J

9 781953 986160